The Homesteader's Daughter

When fifteen-year-old Maybelle Cade and her family joined one of the last wagon trains heading West in 1875, their only aim was to establish a little homestead in Nebraska. They could not have known that they were heading into the middle of a vicious range war which would see them fighting against ruthless and violent men who are determined to drive them from the 160 acres upon which they have settled. So, when a series of confrontations between her father and a local landowner lead inexorably to a bloody climax, young Maybelle faces a notorious killer alone on the Nebraska plains. . . .

The Homesteader's Daughter

Harriet Cade

A Black Horse Western

ROBERT HALE · LONDON

© Simon Webb 2013
First published in Great Britain 2013

ISBN 978-0-7198-0879-1

Robert Hale Limited
Clerkenwell House
Clerkenwell Green
London EC1R 0HT

www.halebooks.com

The right of Simon Webb to be identified as
author of this work has been asserted by him
in accordance with the Copyright, Designs and
Patents Act 1988

Typeset by
Derek Doyle & Associates, Shaw Heath
Printed and bound in Great Britain by
CPI Antony Rowe, Chippenham and Eastbourne

CHAPTER 1

My family, which is to say me, my father and mother and my baby brother, lived in a two room apartment in Pittsburgh. My father worked as an engineer for some big company, but he'd grown up on a farm and starting a farm of his own was what he'd been aiming to do ever since the war ended. He had just somehow not got around to doing it. That's how it is sometimes in this world.

One day while we were eating supper, he says, casual like, 'How'd you all like to live on a farm? Get right away from this dirty city and live in the open air?' My ma seemed kind of dubious. Davy, my brother, being only a year old, was too young to express an opinion, but I said,

'Pa, that's a great idea! When can we go?'

He smiled at me and said, 'We leave Pittsburgh in exactly one month.' Ma pulled a sour face at that, it seeming to her that he hadn't really been consulting us at all, but presenting us with what is known as a *fait accompli.* She said as much, but my father he just laughed, nodded his head at me and told her, 'Maybelle is right pleased at the idea.'

'Well,' said my mother, not a little peevishly, 'In such a case, I wonder that you and she don't just move to this farm by yourselves and leave me and Davy here in Pittsburgh.'

My father caught my eye and as clear as if he had whispered it in my ear, I knew that he wished me to smooth things over a little with Ma. To this end, I reminded her of all the complaints which she had voiced over the years about living in a big, dirty city. After a while she softened and at length said to my father, 'I will allow that there is some merit in the scheme, Ebenezer. Howsoever, I would be greatly obliged if the next time you have any plans of this sort to make, you would first discuss them with me.'

My father did his best to look sheepish and apologetic. 'Martha,' he said, 'I truly thought it would be in the nature of a pleasant surprise for you to be moving away from Pittsburgh. Like Maybelle says, you have had enough to say about this town over the years.'

'Never you mind what Maybelle says. Do not suppose for one moment that it escapes my notice when the two of you combine in this way to bring me round to your opinion.'

There was little that either I or my father could say to that and we both felt it safer to leave the subject alone now, seeing that Ma seemed content with the plan.

For the next month my father and I were all happy and excited, like you are when you're getting ready to go on vacation. My mother was still distinctly cool about the business, seeing as how she hadn't really been given a choice in the matter. The plan was that Pa would send all the money he had saved to an agent in Independence, which was a town on the Missouri river. This man would buy us a covered wagon, fit it out and arrange for us to join a wagon train heading west.

In those days the government would just *give* land to anybody who wanted it. Anyone who asked could be given 160 acres, and the only condition was that you had to go and build a house and actually live on the land. Imagine that, the government giving folk something for nothing! You'd think there had to be some sort of catch and you'd be right, although we didn't find that out until later. The land which my father had claimed was in the Nebraska territory, which as you may know was part of the Great Plains. It would be a journey of about 500 miles from Independence, which my father calculated would take us the best part of a month and a half to complete.

Getting to Independence was not a difficult task; we travelled there by railroad. It was a busy town, though not of course as civilized as Pittsburgh. It was a little rough, but there was plenty of money around. Pa said that the town had grown rich by robbing and cheating all the overlanders who came there to join the wagon trains heading west along the Oregon trail. Be that as it may, a week after we arrived we started out along with fifty other wagons, in the direction of Oregon.

I should at this point say some few words about wagon trains. First off is where there were hardly any horses in the whole enterprise. How's that? I hear you saying. What's this foolishness, a wagon train without *horses*? Yes sir, that's right. No horses at all except half a dozen or so for the scouts who rode on ahead checking out the trail.

The wagons themselves were in the main pulled by oxen and I'll tell you for why. When you claimed that government land, oxen's a sight more use than horses when it comes to ploughing up virgin soil, on account of they have a deal more stamina.

The main disadvantage of oxen is their speed, or I should say their lack of speed. You probably heard about horse racing, but I'll warrant you never heard of oxen racing! I tell you, on a good day those creatures might move about as fast as an old man with the asthma who's carrying a heavy sack up a hill. If we made fifteen miles in a day we thought we were moving at a right smart pace.

Then there's the noise. We all hung everything we didn't want cluttering up the inside of the wagon on hooks fix to the outside. By which I mean pots, pans, buckets, tools and so on. The effect from fifty wagons with no suspension and all that ironmongery bouncing about was purely deafening. You didn't tend to talk much while you was travelling, on account of it meant shouting at the top of your voice.

On top of this is the dust. We travelled not on a road but over what was in essence a mud track. Think on this – fifty wagons drawn by around 200 oxen, all going over a heap of dried mud. By the end of the day, hell, by the end of the *morning*, we were absolutely coated in dust. So if I were to sum up travelling by wagon train I would have to say: slow, noisy and dirty.

Before I carry on with my tale, I should say a word about language. I mean *bad* language – swearing and such. I tell you now, the amount of cursing you heard on the trail is something else and I'm not talking about 'darn' or 'heck', nor even 'damn' and 'hell'. Some of them boys, particularly the scouts, it seemed to me they couldn't string two words together without one of them being 'f***' or 's***'. After a while you just got used to it, but if anybody is offended by such words then they would be best advised to stop reading now.

A week after we started out from Independence I saw a man killed. This was the first time I had ever seen such a thing and it has stuck in my memory. Cursing and bad language played a part in this death, which is why it has come into my mind. This is what happened.

Every wagon was supposed to be in the charge of a grown man. Well, one family came to Independence just like us to start along the Oregon Trail. This family consisted of a man and his wife and their son Jed who was, I suppose, about seventeen years of age. Leastways, I guess he was about that age; I was fifteen and I figure he was two years or so older than me. Howsoever, this family had no sooner arrived in Independence than the man contracted some sort of fever, from which he then proceeded to die. Although it was against the rules, the captain of the wagon train let this woman and her son come along anyway. I think he got paid a certain amount for every wagon he took along the trail and I guess he was reluctant to lose the fee from this wagon.

You might think the boy would have been glad to be allowed along despite his father dying, and would've kept his head down and his mouth shut. Not him. He was the most contentious youth I ever encountered. He was forever interrupting conversations, offering his opinions uninvited and generally making a nuisance of himself. People made allowance for him because his pa had died, but one day he really pissed off one of the scouts. This was during the halt at midday and I happened to be near by. I did not hear what Jed had said, but the scout suddenly exploded, shouting at him in front of everybody, 'Boy, why don't you just shut the f*** up?'

Jed, he was mortified. He particularly disliked being called 'boy'. From what we made out afterwards, what happened next was this. During the rest of the day's driving Jed let his mother handle the team of four oxen while he gave his attention to a bottle of rye whiskey which he had discovered in the wagon. It had probably belonged to his dead pa. Anyways, he commenced to drink most of the bottle, with the natural result that by the time we stopped at sundown he was drunk as a fiddler's bitch.

Whilst we were all setting up camp, Jed came staggering up to the scout who had sworn at him. He could hardly stand, but he was waving around his father's gun, which was a Navy Colt .36 calibre revolver as my father later told me. When the scout, whose name I don't recall, saw Jed he made the mistake of laughing at him, saying, 'Shit, boy. You better put your daddy's gun away till you growed up a bit.' Whereupon Jed shot him in the belly.

Now something that surprised me at the time was that you would expect under such circumstances for blood to begin to flow at once. What happened, though, was just a neat little hole in the scout's shirt, which hardly noticed at all. I'm talking here of course about a bullet from a handgun. A shotgun will make considerably more than a neat little hole, as I discovered for myself later that year when I had occasion to kill a man with one.

In the meantime, the scout is standing there in surprise, clutching his belly and hollering, 'He's killed me. The boy's killed me.' Jed is still waving this pistol around and people are diving to the ground and hiding behind wagons in case he takes it into his head to shoot somebody else. Then he turns in my direction, not meaning me any harm, I think, but kind of dazed with the liquor and hardly knowing what he was doing. It was however enough for my father who, perceiving as he saw it a threat to his family, jumped on Jed from behind and knocked him to the ground. Then he grabs Jed's hair and bangs his head up and down vigorously on the ground until he has knocked him out.

I never knew a man to make such a production out of dying as that scout. It was plain to everyone as set eyes on his wound that he was done for, there not being a doctor for many miles in any direction. He spent the whole evening and most of the night wailing and complaining about his fate. He was shouting, 'Oh, God I don't want to die!' and 'Lord, I ain't ready to come to you yet!' and similar things. It was specially ironic seeing as how this man had been a notorious hard drinker and gambler, the last person you would have suspicioned to have been worrying about the afterlife! My father said it was right heart-warming to hear such a profane roughneck turn to religion in this way. I think he was joking. However the novelty wore off and by midnight folk had had enough of it and were wishing he'd just die peaceably and let the rest of us get some sleep, which he finally did, but not until it was nearly dawn.

And that is the true story of how bad language caused a man's death. If the scout had asked that boy politely, 'Excuse me young man, would you mind remaining silent for a few moments?' instead of shouting and cursing, then he most likely would not have got shot.

Next morning they buried the deceased man, which is to say they scraped a hole two inches deep and laid him there with a load of rocks piled on him. My father said he figured that as soon as we left there, the coyotes would dig up the body and pull it to pieces.

As for Jed, since nobody was fond enough of the dead man to avenge him, the captain of the wagon train decided to call it an accident. However, he wasn't none too enthusiastic on the idea of travelling another 1,000 miles in the company of a boy prone to accidentally discharging firearms, so he directed Jed and his mother to return to Independence alone and he would consider the matter closed. Which they did.

Two more people died before we split off from the wagon train and went north towards Dakota. One was a woman with the bloody flux – what you would now call cholera. The other was a little boy who simply died in his sleep. His parents would not at first bury him, but wanted to take his body with them to Oregon and bury him by their new home. They changed their minds later when the corpse began decomposing and liquefying. People near to them complained about the smell when we camped and they were obliged to bury him out on the prairie anyway. My personal opinion is that they would have done better to bury that child before he turned all mushy and began stinking the place out.

Most of the wagons in this train were heading across the Rocky Mountains, where some would proceed to Oregon and others to California. Seven or eight however were, like us, going to settle in Nebraska or Wyoming. We cut across Kansas, entered Nebraska and followed the Platte River. Somewhere near a town called Bayard we split off from the rest of the wagon train and headed north in order to make our own individual ways to our destinations. In our case this was a small valley through which ran a tributary of the Niobrara River.

Four of these other families which were heading in roughly the same direction as us were black. Some of the homesteaders where we settled were black, as were a lot of the cowboys and soldiers whom we encountered. Speaking for myself, I have never noticed any particular difference between a black man and a white man. I have know many scoundrelly white men and also a lot of reliable and industrious black men. And of course vice versa. I never noticed that the colour of their skin affected their disposition in any particular way.

Perhaps you would like to hear about life on the trail? Well, all I can say is, it was just terrible. We were up at dawn and travelling with one stop till nightfall. I say with one stop, but I mean to suggest with one *planned* stop. What with axles breaking, the occasional ox dying, accidents, fords impassable due to swollen rivers and I don't know what all else, there were certainly more stops than just that scheduled one at midday for our meal.

Now this isn't a travel book nor yet a geography lesson. I don't expect you want to know the name of every

13

damned flower on that prairie, or what the Indians called various things. I cannot stand that sort of thing in a book. Somebody gave me a book for my birthday a couple of years back. It was called something like *Legends of the Old West* or some such nonsense. Every page had words in various Indian languages and a whole heap of asterixes at the bottom of the page explaining what they all meant. It was full of stuff like; *In the spring the obajiboos* dug mogawoga* roots and then pounded them to make Flobadom**. Well I can tell you right now, there won't be any of that foolishness here. All I will say is that there were a lot of little flowers on the prairies, some of which were red and some yellow. I guess that's all the information any normal person would be requiring on that subject.

One thing does stick in my mind and that was gathering fuel for to cook the evening meal. Would you care to guess what we used to cook with? I will tell you. Buffalo shit! Yes, that's right. Every time we stopped to make camp, I had to fetch the wheelbarrow out the back of the wagon and trundle off across the plain in competition with fifty other people to gather enough buffalo shit to build a fire. In the history books about that time which I have seen they refer to 'buffalo chips', but I do not recollect any such reticence on the subject at the time. We knew all right that we was picking up shit.

I must say a few words regarding the sort of country we were travelling through after we entered Nebraska. Some early travellers described these areas as deserts, but this is not accurate although there is certainly a resemblance. As far as the horizon, all you could see was grass and, it being springtime, there was, as I mentioned above, a scattering of pretty little flowers. Hardly any trees, no mountains, pretty well nothing but miles and miles of grass.

I said to Pa, 'I thought you said we was going to build us a house when we arrive. How we going to do that without any wood? Are there trees on our land or are we aiming to buy in some lumber?' I suppose I was thinking of some species of log cabin, like the kind of place where Abe Lincoln was raised.

'Why you think we need wood to build a house?' he asked me.

'Well, are we going to use bricks then?' I enquired.

'Nothing of the sort.' he replied, smiling to hisself.

'Then it's going to be like those old Israelites, I guess, making bricks without straw.'

'You are a right smart girl, Maybelle,' he exclaimed. 'That is exactly what it will be like.'

My father would not be drawn any more on this particular subject. He was, as you might say, a man who played his cards close to his chest. He did not confide in anybody much, not even my mother.

Shortly after leaving Bayard we separated from the other half dozen wagons and went our own individual way. Couple of days later we reached a railroad line which was as I recall something to do with the Union Pacific line. At any event, I remember my father telling me that it ran to Cheyenne. Alongside the tracks was a telegraph line strung up along tall poles, from one of which hung a man's body.

My father stopped the wagon and contemplated this

sight for a space. The man had evidently been dead for a while, because a crowd of flies were buzzing round his face. He was suspended by the neck and a large square of pasteboard had been somehow affixed to his chest. On it was printed the word THIEF.

Pa pulled out his pipe, filled and lit it, not taking his eyes from the corpse, while my mother made various observations along the lines of 'How terrible!' and 'Lordy, what a dreadful thing to see!'

'What do you make of this here, Maybelle?' my father asked.

'Well, I never knew thieving was a hanging matter,' I replied.

'You think this fellow was hung up by a court?'

'You mean he was lynched? I thought only black men got lynched.'

'I'll lay odds that this matter is related to rustling cattle, or what they call stock theft in these parts,' my father opined, nodding to hisself.

Now I must tell you, in retrospect as it were, that what was going on here was what they called a range war. You are most likely scratching your head at this point, saying to yourself, 'I have heard tell of these "range wars" before, but I have no clear understanding of what is meant by the expression.' I shall explain.

All the land in that territory, right up into Dakota and as far as the Canadian border, rightly belonged to the government. That was, as you might say, theoretically the case and it was why the government was so free and easy about giving it to folks like us. Howsoever, a lot of big ranchers and cattlemen used that same land to graze their cattle on. They had thousands and thousands of cattle and consequently needed a whole heap of land to keep them fed and watered. These men were very powerful and influential locally and they felt that the government in Washington were sufficiently distant from them that they did not need to pay overmuch attention to what all those senators and congressmen in Washington was saying. In other words, they felt that they were 'A law unto themselves'.

So when the government encouraged settlers to move in and take that land and start cultivating it, the cattleman saw it in the light of losing something belonging to *them*. What irked them most was where the new arrivals, my father included, tended naturally to want land next to a ready supply of water – rivers and streams. Meant not having to dig a well, you see. This of course made life a little tedious if you was running a herd of 1,000 head or so of cattle and were looking for them all to drink their fill. All those little farmers putting up fences and blocking access to the water, the ranchers called this losing their 'water rights'.

Now a thing which I have observed many times over the years is that no sooner do one set of men commence talking of their 'rights' than another set will appear who begin to complain of their 'wrongs'. Presently the two parties fall to disputing and before you know it trouble develops. Depending upon circumstances, this trouble can take the form of anything from a fistfight to a world war. The affair into which we were about to become involved fell somewhere between these two extremes.

CHAPTER 2

So there we were, stuck in the middle of the damned prairie with not a tree in sight, nearest town four miles away and only a wagon to sleep under. Just as I did then, you are probably wondering to yourself, how the hell are they going to build a house? It was a genuine conundrum, the answer to which was known only to my father.

Next morning my father got up and while Ma was preparing breakfast, he said, 'Give me a hand, Maybelle, I want to get that plough down off the wagon.'

'The plough!' I exclaimed. 'What in the hell do you want with the plough, Pa? I thought we was building a house today?'

'Not so much of the "hell", young lady. We are so going to build a house, but first we have to do us a little ploughing.'

Well, it sounded crazy to me, but I went along with it and after breakfast I helped hitch up the oxen to our shiny new plough. While we did so, my mother sat on the ground, nursing the baby and looking right dispirited. She really did not look like a woman who was taking to all this pioneer business. Looked to me as though she was wishing herself back in Pittsburgh.

My father ploughed a long, straight furrow and then stopped. One thing you have to understand about soil on the prairie is that it is not the loose, crumbly earth such as you get in your garden when you are digging. The roots from all them tough grasses extend in a thick mat going down maybe two or three feet. The result is that when you first plough, digging into the soil and turning it over, you end up with a long, thick, solid, rectangular block of roots mixed with soil.

After ploughing this one furrow, Pa goes back to the wagon and fetches a big wood saw. 'Think you can use this without sawing off your fingers or nothing?' he ask me.

'I know how to use a saw,' I said, a little affronted like.

'Then start sawing up this here cable of earth. We want lengths of two foot or so. Try and make them all the same size.'

'Hey Pa, it's just like I said. We're making bricks without straw.'

By midday we had produced in this way dozens of bricks of root and earth, each one two feet long, a foot wide and perhaps six or eight inches deep. After a light dinner of porridge and coffee, my father laid out with string the outline of a house. Really, it was no more than a large hut, but we called it our house.

My mother put little Davy down for a nap in the wagon and the three of us proceeded to hump those earthen blocks into place, so laying the first course of the walls. This is what was called a sod house, or soddy for short, and it is what most of the homesteaders in that district lived in when they arrived. After a while the roots grew and tangled together and it was all fairly secure, provided that you didn't try and build the walls too high. Mark you, the earth was just full of various creatures which you would not willingly share your home with, such as spiders, snakes, worms and a variety of bugs. Not to mention the occasional mouse. Even after it was completed, these living things would continue to regard the walls of your house as a natural extension of the prairie, which led to many amusing scenes.

To cut a long story short, we built our 'house' and it took us less than a week to do so, during which time it only rained twice, which was fortunate for us. When it was finished my father fixed up a roof with a couple of rolls of tarred paper which he had brought along from Independence. The windows were nothing more than narrow slits and the doorway was simply that, an opening with no door in it.

Throughout the entire process, I still detected what you might term a lack of enthusiasm from my mother. This continued right up until we had finished the actual building and were moving in. I found this strange, because as I saw it this would surely beat sleeping in the open under a wagon. But then, when you are fifteen I guess everything is a kind of adventure. The whole business of moving to Nebraska and building this hut was like one big vacation to me, especially as it was looking to me like I'd finished with school for good.

Our new home did not boast much in the way of decoration, apart from an old Indian blanket which we hung in the doorway to keep out the draught. Truth to tell, we didn't have much to speak of in the way of furniture either. Hell, what am I saying? We didn't have any furniture. You ever hear the saying: *they were so poor, they didn't have a pot to piss in?* Well, sir, that was us. God's honest truth, we didn't have a pot to piss in. Pa just dug a hole a way from the house and that's what we used for calls of nature.

Just about the only thing we had to decorate the walls with was an old fowling piece. This was a double-barrelled, muzzle-loading shotgun with which my father aimed to provide us with meat for the pot. As soon as the tar-paper roof was in place, he loaded this gun and hung it proudly on the wall. This was safer than it might sound because, like most firearms at that time, our shotgun was single action. This meant that before pulling the trigger, you first had to pull back the hammer and cock it. With this particular type of gun it was also necessary to fit little copper percussion caps under the hammer before it could fire. Mark you, weapons like that can be mighty temperamental. This is because the notch that catches inside the mechanism when you cock such a gun can get worn down with use. You are apt to end up with what is known as a 'hair trigger'. I have known guns like that, some of them so sensitive that they will go off when cocked if somebody in the vicinity so much as sneezes or farts.

We got that tar-paper fixed up around mid-morning, and as soon as we had secured it we all sat down and finished off the remains of our breakfast porridge. Now if this were a movie or a storybook, then the next few weeks or so would consist of what you might term a rural idyll. My father would plant his wheat, while Ma baked wholesome food and I frolicked in the Nebraska sun. Friendly Indians would come to trade and we would attend barn dances in the nearby town. Any sort of trouble would not occur for at least another twenty pages and it would all build up gradually.

Well, I can only tell you what really happened and what happened was that within fifteen minutes of getting that tar-paper up, trouble purely came knocking on our door. This is how it went that day.

While we were relishing our cold porridge we became aware of a figure that appeared over the grassy ridge about half a mile from us. As it approached at a run, we could see that it was a colored boy about the same age as me. He looked to be in a pitiable condition, for as he reached us we could hear him gasping and whimpering with fear and distress. He kind of collapsed in front of us, gabbling in an exceedingly thick accent that, 'Dey gonna kill me!'

My father remained as calm and unflustered as always. 'Nobody's going to kill you, son,' he said kindly. 'Come on in the house and let's see what's what.' We all went indoors and as I glanced back I said to my father,

'Pa, somebody's heading this way!' which triggered off a paroxysm of sobbing and moaning from the young black man. From the same direction as that the coloured boy had come, I could see two riders heading towards us.

'Dey sho' gonna kill me!' he muttered, starting to weep.

'Nobody will kill you,' said my father calmly. 'You all

stay in here now. I will handle this.'

He reached down his shotgun unhurriedly and cocked both hammers, slipping percussion caps over the nipples. Then he walked out and waited for the two riders who were now less than a hundred yards way. As they got closer I waited till my mother turned to pour out a cup of coffee for the boy, then I slipped outside to see what would happen.

The two men who reined in their horses a few yards from my father looked very different from each other. One was a pale, middle-aged man, say forty or fifty years of age. He was running to fat and dressed far too smartly to be riding the range. It looked to me like he had jumped on his horse in a hurry in response to some emergency. Whatever had happened did not seem to have put him in an agreeable frame of mind. He looked exceedingly bad-tempered. By way of contrast, the other man, who was younger, looked as if he *lived* on horseback. He was thin and wiry and burned brown by being outside in the sun so much. I never saw a man with bluer eyes, that stood out in that brown, weathered face like two jewels in a dunghill. He was wearing a gunbelt and also had a rifle in a saddle holster in front of him. He was a hard one all right and you got the clear impression that he would use those weapons just as easy as he would light a cigarette.

They did not bother with any of the usual civilities, such as 'Good morning' or 'How do you do?' The older man looked around and tried to peer through the door of our 'house', which I could see irritated my father. Then he stared at my father coldly and without introducing hisself or offering any explanation said, 'Have you seen a young buck anyways around here?'

'Now who might you be and why are you asking?' my father said in a friendly fashion.

The two men kind of stiffened, as though they were unused to being spoken to in such a confident fashion. The one who had asked my father about the black man, he began to swell up like a toad.

'You had best not fool with me,' he said. 'Just answer my question yes or no; have you seen a young black man in the last half-hour or so?'

Instead of replying directly my father said mildly, 'We have not met before and neither of you has yet favoured me with your name, but I'll be free with mine. I am Ebenezer Cade. You might not know that all this land, down as far as yonder river, is mine and I have to say I don't take overmuch to being questioned in this way while I am on my own property. Unless either of you is a lawman, which I would take oath is not the case. Still and all, I should be sorry to be at outs with my neighbours so soon after moving here.'

'*Neighbours?*' said the pudgy man incredulously, 'Do you think for one moment that I look upon you damned squatters as my *neighbours*? Hell!' The younger man gave a short, ugly laugh which sounded like the bark of an angry dog. Then he hawked and spat, the thick phlegm splattering down near my father's boots. The other man, he who was well dressed, said, 'I take it you would have no objection to us looking inside that mud hut of yours?'

'Well,' said my father,' we have only just finished building it and it is none too tidy inside. Howsoever, if you would care to return in a week or so, I should be right happy to invite you in and offer you a bite to eat. But in the meantime I would be ashamed to have anybody see inside, so the answer will have to be no.'

He stood relaxed and easy, with the shotgun held loose under his arm, not aimed at the men, but obviously cocked and ready. Young as I was, it was plain to me that if any trouble started, then my pa would be able to bring up that shotgun and let fly with both barrels before anybody else would even have time to draw a weapon. I imagine the very same thought had occurred to the two men, because they neither of them made any sudden movements that might have been open to misinterpretation. Instead, the older one leaned forward slowly in the saddle and glared at my father.

'You would be making a very big mistake if you was to get crosswise to me,' he said.

My father appeared to consider this statement seriously for a moment or two before saying thoughtfully, 'It may be as you say, that I am making a mistake of that sort. It would not be the first time in my life and it probably won't be the last.'

'I would not count on that,' said the man. 'Which is to say that this may well prove to be the last mistake you ever make.' He and my father looked at each other for a few seconds. Then the rider turned his horse round and set off at a canter, back the way he had come. The other man, he with the bright blue eyes, did not at once follow, but stared at my father as though hoping to memorize his face. Pa just stood there staring right back at him, relaxed and easy as could be. At length, this man too rode off.

'That was great, Pa,' I told him. 'You just stood there like you weren't affeared of nothing.'

'Any man tell you that in such circumstances he has no fear, then he is either a liar or a mad fool. I had fear all right.'

'Then how come you didn't give way?'

'I will tell you, Maybelle, that in such cases what you must do is simply to stand your ground. Don't move forward, aggressive like, or start yelling. I have seen men that was on the point of running away, panicked into fighting because somebody advanced upon them. No, you just stand there and in ninety nine cases out of a hundred you will hold the field.'

'What happens on the hundredth occasion?'

'Have I not always said that you are a right smart girl, Maybelle Louise?' he said, smiling and ruffling my hair as he did sometimes when he was pleased with me. 'That is exactly the question to ask. The answer is that when you are doing your standing firm, it helps to have a shotgun in your hands. And then, should it prove to be the hundredth time when nobody will back down, well under such circumstances someone is apt to get killed. And if you have a loaded shotgun in your hands and it is cocked and primed, then it probably won't be you who is killed.'

My mother, who had come out quietly without either of us noticing, exploded at that point, saying, 'Why are you filling that child's head with a lot of foolishness about standing her ground and killing people? It would be more to the point if she learnt to sew and bake rather more than she does at the moment.'

My father winked at me and we went into the house to see what we could do for the young black man whose name turned out to be Ikey. I will not write down what that boy told us verbatim because there was much repetition, interspersed with frequent protestations of innocence. Also, his accent was thick and his speech larded with curious words and turns of phrase. What it amounted to was this:

The older, pale fellow who had called on us owned a big ranch near by. He pastured and watered his cattle in this area and was getting tired of outsiders settling along the river choking him off from his 'water rights'. The nearest lawman was maybe fifteen miles away, so Anderson, the owner of the ranch, was pretty well having it all his own way. Less than a week before we arrived, one of the homesteaders along the river had been accused of rustling and after some species of trial had been strung up. It was seemingly his body we had seen hanging from the telegraph pole. Ikey, the coloured boy, said that things were getting so lively that some of the homesteaders were considering moving somewhere a little quieter. The reason Anderson had been on his trail was that Ikey had come across a newborn calf which was unbranded, what you call a 'maverick'. By tradition, such unbranded steers were regarded as being anybody's, finders keepers as you might say. Unfortunately he had been seen by one of Anderson's cowboys, who had raised a hue and cry, which led to Anderson and his foreman tracking Ikey to our house.

My father listened quietly to all this, and then set off to escort Ikey home, just in case Anderson and his men were planning to ambush him when he left us. I wanted to go as well, just to meet our neighbours as it were, but my father would not hear of it.

It was just after dark by the time my father returned and he was none too forthcoming about what, if anything, he had learned from our new neighbours. Like I said earlier, he was a man who played his cards close to his chest. Anyways, there was not time for much talking as we was all pretty beat and ready to sleep. Before this, we all sat down for prayers.

It was not at all singular in those days for a family to pray together. My father, though, seemed to have a specially close relationship with the Almighty compared with other people we knew. My mother was Catholic and for festivals such as Easter and Christmas we attended a Catholic church in Pittsburgh. For the folk at that church the Lord seemed to be a very powerful and important but essentially remote personage, rather like the President in Washington DC. When my father prayed, however, you felt like the Almighty was right there in the room with you. He was respectful, but not humble and spoke to God man to man without mincing his words none. If he felt that the Lord had overlooked something or was screwing up, well then it was Pa's business to set him straight and remind him of the exact details of his covenant with us.

'Lord,' my father would say bluntly, 'it seems to me that you are allowing the ungodly to flourish a mite too freely round here, not to mention where some of the righteous ain't doing as well as they might. For instance, there's your servant, Grover Johnson – a God-fearing man if ever I knew one. He's lost his job and him with a family to feed and all. It appears to me that you'd be wanting to do something about that and pretty quick.'

When we lived in Pittsburgh a group of men used to meet at our apartment to pray and read the Bible. They all, like my father, seemed on intimate terms with the Deity and often reminded him of where he seemed to be falling down on the job. Growing up, I gained the distinct impression that if my father and his friends weren't always on hand with regular guidance and advice, then the Lord would be forever getting himself in a muddle and losing sight of his various duties and responsibilities.

Tonight, Pa kept it short and to the purpose. 'Lord, we thank You for sending young Ikey to us in his hour of need and I am mighty obliged to You for not sending him 'til I had my twelve gauge loaded and ready to hand. Amen.' After which we all snuggled down on our blankets and slept the sleep of the just until the following morning.

CHAPTER 3

I feel the time has come to say a few words about my family. I do not mean what colour their eyes were or the clothes they wore or how their hair was fixed or anything at all of that kind. Rather, I aim to tell you what sort of people they were, which I am sure you will find a deal more interesting.

My father was what I would describe as a gentle man. These days, calling a man 'gentle' is next door to branding him as a homosexual, but I do not wish at all to convey the idea that he was in any way soft or weak. As you will already have observed, when it came right down to the nitty gritty my pa would bow to nobody. When I say he was gentle I mean to say that he was not one for shouting, brag or bluster. He always spoke carefully and quietly and if it chanced that he had to act, well then he did so without saying overmuch about the matter either before or after the event.

Something I should mention is that my father had spent above four years in the Union army. His family were real religious, Quakers or some such and also

30

staunch abolitionists. I gather that he joined up in April 1861 when Mr Lincoln called for volunteers after the shelling of Fort Sumter. His joining the army was as a matter of principle, seeing as how he and his family were so against slavery. Pa would never talk to us about the war and about the only thing I know for sure is that he was commissioned 'in the field' for some conspicuous act of bravery. He ended the war as a captain. He was not a man to cross lightly, as Anderson had discovered.

I do not recollect my father ever raising his voice to me, much less striking me. Which I have to say was most unusual in those days. If he was vexed with me, he would shake his head sadly and say, 'Maybelle, I am right disappointed in you. I thought better of you,' or something similar. Such words, coupled with the look in his eyes, were enough to reduce me to tears.

My mother was a pretty woman. Her given name was Martha and she was a little over thirty years of age that year but looked considerable younger. She was, I am afraid, not an intelligent person and it showed in the things she said and her general demeanour. Child-like would about sum up her character. My father, although he had received little formal schooling, was intelligent and as I grew older he fell into the way of talking to and confiding in me rather than my mother. As you may well imagine, this made things a little tense at times between the three of us. I was fond enough of Ma, but my father meant everything to me. As I have already remarked, my little brother did not take much part in the events I am narrating, on account of he did very little at that time except eat, shit and cry.

A couple of days after his run in with Anderson, my father said to me one morning, 'Well, young Maybelle, feel like a trip into town?' I needed no second bidding and we set off to walk into town.

At this point I feel that some of you are probably saying to yourselves, 'Hmmm, what about the child's mother, to say nothing of the baby? Ain't they getting to visit town too?' Well, all I can say is that that's how it was in our family at that time, Pa and me making one set and my mother and the baby another. As I said before, this did make for a certain amount of contention in my relations with my Ma, but there it was.

One reason that I was so glad to be visiting town was that those first days after we had built our house were very exhausting. My father had been ploughing the prairie up as fast as he could, with a view to planting his seed. You have no idea how hard that earth was. I have already said that it was good enough to make bricks from, which gives you some notion of what it would be like to try and plant anything in such soil. Here is what we were doing for those days. My father would rise at first light and plough a few furrows. Then he would take a spade and break up the turned earth with a spade. I would follow behind with a basket and collect any large stones. This work was back breaking and discouraging, because it was not even certain that the seed we sowed was going to grow.

I ought to say here that this was one more reason why big ranchers like Anderson sometimes didn't have too much trouble in driving away small farmers like us. This kind of farming, on desolate and barren soil, is a soul-destroying business and after a year or so of struggling many families were just about ready to throw in their hand without the extra problem of threats of violence. Anyways, speaking for myself, after three or four days of this work I was surely ready for a break.

Not only was I very tired of working in the field, but after weeks of seeing pretty well nothing but grass while we were travelling to this place, the prospect of visiting even the smallest town was, as you might imagine, an attractive one to a lively fifteen-year-old girl. We walked there and it took us a little over an hour to do so.

The nearest town to our little homestead was called Zion and it was about four miles from us. Incidentally, you won't find Zion in any atlas of the USA, so don't bother looking. Hundreds of little towns were springing up all over the place like mushrooms at that time. Those which flourished and grew were generally the ones beside railroads and in this respect Zion had already 'missed the boat'. Some ten miles in the other direction to us from Zion was another little town and this town more or less straddled the railroad which we had crossed to reach our farm. It was this town which grew and today boasts some tens of thousands of inhabitants. Others, like Zion, withered away and became ghost towns. There's hardly a trace of many of those places today, only shadows in the wheat when the sun is low on the horizon.

Here is what the town of Zion looked like at that time. As you walked into town you passed various dwelling houses, about half of them soddies of the type which we had ourselves lately built. These were all single-storey constructions and I suppose that they were thrown up by the first settlers to the area, although they looked to be still inhabited.

As you got closer to the main street of the town, the buildings were bigger and made of wood. The biggest was a saloon which was three storeys high, the top two floors being a whorehouse. In addition to this there was a livery stable, blacksmith, church, general store and so on. I don't rightly know how many folk lived there at that time but I should say it must have amounted to some hundreds.

When we first got to town my father insisted that I walk along of him, but after ten minutes or so it all seemed quiet and peaceful enough and he yielded to my entreaties and allowed me to go off and explore by myself. He said he had some business at the livery stable and told me not to get into any sort of mischief.

I wandered round for a space, looking at things in general before going into the general store. There didn't seem to be much of interest there, it being full of such things as bales of cloth, tools, lamp oil and various other dull items. Besides which, I didn't have so much as a cent to my name and so however interesting the wares I wasn't in the market for buying them. As I made to leave the store a dishevelled, uncouth-looking young man with bright red, carroty hair was entering. He smelled strongly of barnyard and whiskey. Instead of stepping aside politely to let me pass, he just stopped dead in the doorway, so as to block the way and prevent me from leaving. He ran his eyes over me in what I would describe as a lascivious manner.

'Weeell,' he exclaimed, 'What have we here? Ain't seen you before and that's a fact. Lemme tell you, I never forgets a pretty face!'

'Let me pass, please,' I told him shortly.

'What's the hurry, little sister? Why don't we get ourselves acquainted like?'

Even in those far off days as a young girl, I was not prone to blushing and simpering and I never could abide a drunken fool, so I said right sharp, 'Get the hell out of my way, you varmint!'

'Ooh, ooh, such language!' he cried, cringing in make-believe horror at my words. He was so busy with this little piece of play-acting that he didn't notice my father coming up behind him. Fact is, while he was pretending to back away in fear of my harsh words he bumped straight into my father, who put his hand on the fellow's shoulder in an amiable and friendly fashion.

'Strikes me,' said my father affably, 'as a young man like you is a mite old to be playing with little girls.' The drunk looked at him in a puzzled way. 'Tell me,' my father asked, 'would you care to try your luck with me?' He asked this as though he were inviting the young man to pitch horseshoes with him. It took the drunk man a second or two to catch the drift, but he eventually realized that, despite his quiet words and pleasant manner, my father was pretty pissed at him for troubling me. Once the penny had dropped, as they say, he shook his head and backed slowly away from my father, keeping a wary eye on him the while. 'You mind how you go now,' Pa called after him, still in that same friendly voice.

We turned back into the store and Pa bought me a bright-yellow hair ribbon. Do you know what? I still have that hair ribbon to this very day! Yes, sir, ninety years later

I have kept it safe, though it has now faded to a pale fawn. It is exceedingly precious to me for a reason which I shall later relate.

After leaving the store my father took me to the livery stable, where he showed me a fine golden palomino gelding. 'What do you think to him, Maybelle?' he enquired.

I stroked his mane and he nuzzled me. 'Pa, he's lovely.'

'Well, he's ours.'

'You bought a horse? How'd you know he's all right? I never thought you knew anything about horses.'

He laughed at this. 'Hell's afire, Maybelle Louise, I was in the Third Kentucky Horse better than two years. If I did not know about horses you think they woulda kept me there all that time and making me a Captain into the bargain, in charge of a troop of a hundred men? Let me tell you, I knows about horses. Not to mention where I growed up on a farm. Soon as they saddle him up we're taking him straight home with us.'

Pa called our new horse 'Dollar'. The reason for this, as he explained to me, was that a good palomino should be just the colour of a newly minted gold dollar. Which, in the pale May sun, was just exactly how he looked to me and as I remember him now.

After the horse was saddled up we headed back to our home, sometimes with Pa on the horse and me walking and then, after I had begged and pleaded with him, he let me get on by myself while he led the horse. Growing up in a big city, I had never ridden on a horse before and it was a great novelty to me.

Back home, my mother had been doing her best to get our house in shape. She had swept the earth floor and strewn it with Montana feathers, (which is to say: straw). She had also made a beginning at digging a patch at the front in order to start a vegetable garden. This was tough work, armed only with a spade, but she was doing OK. Ikey's mother had called by and left some cooked food, presumably as a token of gratitude for what Pa had done. After we had eaten the food, my mother expressed a wish to take a ride on the horse. She was in a playful mood, not common with her, and so my father quickly obliged by lifting her on to the palomino's back. Her long skirts were all in the way and she was laughing and blushing. After my father had set her on the horse, he stood back and laughed as well. I can see that face of his now, smiling in appreciation of the ridiculous spectacle that my mother presented on the horse in that long skirt all rucked up so's you could see her petticoats and drawers.

Memory is a very strange and unreliable thing, especially as you get older. I have the most vivid memory of the expression on my father's face on a May afternoon nigh on a century ago, but I have trouble recalling what I ate for lunch yesterday. I guess that this may in general be because there is nothing much *worth* remembering these days, passing my days as I do among a crowd of grey ghosts, half of whom would not even wipe their arse unless reminded to do so. Maybe I try to forget about this current life of mine and retreat into the pleasanter memories of my youth and childhood.

Anyhows, who in the hell would care to hear stories

about what I see and do in this damned place? The old man who sits opposite me at mealtimes muttering 'terrible' and 'absolutely disgraceful' under his breath the whole time. Or the woman who comes up to everybody a dozen times a day and asks, 'Is my daughter coming today?' I never yet seen that old woman get a single visitor. I dare say her own flesh and blood find her just as annoying as the rest of us. Like I say, hardly worth remembering. But the sun over those Nebraska plains that spring or the palomino my pa bought that first day we went to Zion, now *those* are surely worth recollecting.

Now that he had a horse my father proposed visiting the other homesteaders up and down the valley, with a view to assessing the situation and figuring out what was the best way to deal with Anderson and his aggressive attitude towards us and the other settlers. I heard him late that night talking to my mother, telling her that what he had gathered from talking to Ikey's step-pa was that Anderson was guying up his activities as a 'vigilance committee'. I had never heard this expression before and I don't suppose you have either. However, I dare say that you will have heard of the abbreviation for such a committee, which is 'vigilantes'.

Now the very word 'vigilante' has today an unsavoury feel about it. Puts you in mind of lynch mobs and the Ku Klux Klan and similar, I dare say. Time was though when vigilantes served a useful purpose. Think on this: living in a rough frontier town with the nearest lawman maybe thirty miles away. Sometimes a posse of bullies and roughnecks could get above themselves and pretty much take over such a town. When this sort of thing happened, it seemed natural and right for decent and law-abiding citizens to band together and run the bad guys out of town.

So far, so good. But if you're not pretty damned careful, these schemes can get out of hand mighty fast. One day you string up a murderer or rapist, the next you're hanging rustlers and then before you know where you are you've hung a man for spitting on the sidewalk. Don't laugh, I tell you I have seen these things happen. Let me tell you a true story to illustrate what I mean.

This happened in a small town with no sheriff but a very active and well organized vigilance committee. They had driven out all the seriously bad elements like the rustlers, thieves, card-sharps and so on. This had been achieved by hanging a few and beating others. The town was nicely cleaned up to the point where they could maintain order simply by handing out the occasional beating to any disreputable types who were threatening to lower the tone of the place in any respect.

Now one local drunk left the saloon in broad daylight and had a call of nature, which he answered in the space between two buildings. After he had made water, but before he had had time to 'adjust his dress', the wife and young daughter of a prominent member of the local vigilance committee chanced by and happened to see him all exposed like. When she told her husband he was so incensed that he collected a few friends and called on the drunk that same night. They began by just knocking him around a bit, but they got a little over-excited, with the consequence that the fellow died the next day of his injuries. Imagine that! Being beaten to death because you were caught short in the street.

What was happening in our particular neighbourhood was that Anderson and some of his men were representing themselves as the local law and order and handing out summary justice to those they claimed to be rustlers, thieves and suchlike. Fact that these folk were standing in his way was just by the by! Anderson was shrewd enough to limit the activities of his vigilantes to the open country and not try to dominate the town itself. This meant that as far as people in the town were concerned, what happened five, six or seven miles outside the town was in the nature of a private quarrel between the homesteaders and Anderson, a quarrel that they were happy to stand aside from if at all possible.

From all that I could collect from what my father was saying, some of the men who had settled near us were wondering whether the best tack to take might not be to band together in their own interests in order to protect themselves from Anderson and his vigilantes. This was, from all points of view, likely to prove a very delicate undertaking and I'll tell you for why. In the first place, nobody in the town had any wish to be caught between and betwixt two bands of armed men at odds with one another. Obvious, really. Secondly, as it says in the Good Book, 'All those who live by the sword shall die by the sword.' Which is to say, suppose such a body, when once formed, proved inferior in courage and firepower to their adversaries? Why, then Anderson would be able to run the whole parcel of them out of the valley! And then again, of course, having fairly recently settled one civil war, the Federal Government in Washington was apt to come down pretty sharpish on anything that looked likely to escalate into an armed conflict. Nobody wanted a troop of soldiers descending on the district to restore order.

So there it was. The people in the town were in a sense caught between Anderson and the homesteaders. On the one hand Anderson was by far and away the richest and most powerful man for many miles around. On the other hand, us homesteaders represented the future; a settled patchwork of farms and smallholdings which would in time grow into a prosperous agricultural community.

It was a tricksy balancing act for the inhabitants of Zion. It was true that Anderson's men spent freely, but they were as rough as all get out and push. Apart from spending money, there was shooting, drunkenness, the odd case of rape and the occasional lynching. Single men, pretty much all they were interested in when they came town was getting liquored up and chasing women. The homesteaders certainly had less cash money to throw around and what they did spend was chiefly on such items as lumber and grain. This caused another division in the town, because the saloon keepers, livery-stable owners and those running the cathouse thought everything was just fine and dandy. They just could not see how a bunch of dirt farmers like us would bring any advantage to them either now or in the future. The other store owners and a large number of townsfolk could however see that a lot of sober, hardworking family men would be a better prospect in the long run than a set of drunken cowboys.

This balancing of immediate short-term gain with

future stability and profit was a calculation being made in countless other small communities across the West at that time. My father had sized the matter up very quickly, as he related to my mother while I lay supposedly asleep.

'Those cowboys that are spending their money in the town, they don't have any roots. Today they spend money, tomorrow they will smash up the saloon while drunk, molest some man's wife or move to another town. Only a fool would rely upon them as a steady source of income. They might buy a quart of rye this month, but they will not return week after week for lamp oil, seed, spades and suchlike, the way that farmers are apt to.'

My mother followed his line of thought well enough, but she was less certain about the case. 'Not everybody plans like you, Ebenezer, looking deep into the future. For a man running a saloon, it is enough if he sells plenty of whiskey. It is nothing to him who is doing the buying of it.'

'This too is true,' agreed my father. 'Still and all, folks all want the same thing when once they have reached a certain age. They want a safe and quiet place to raise their families. Even the saloon owner most likely has a wife and children. He will not want a bunch of drunken cowboys shooting up his town. He would sooner have steady men coming in each week for a few drinks and leaving in an orderly fashion. I see that there will be gunplay and disorder in that town before long, at least from what I have been hearing. Nobody wishes to live under such conditions.'

My mother seemed unconvinced and their talk kind of petered out until they fell asleep.

CHAPTER 4

I shall now attempt a description of the geography of our corner of Nebraska at that time. If I do not do so, then nobody will be likely to understand much of what follows. The morning after we went to Zion, I asked Pa if I could go off and visit our neighbours.

'It's nothing to me,' he told me. 'So if'n your Ma can spare you and you don't make a nuisance of yourself, I don't see why not.'

'Yes,' said Ma. 'And if that is not just like you, Ebenezer Cade. You think that I will keep house, cook, look after Davy and all, while your little princess goes skipping off the Lord knows where. Well, I'm here to tell you that neither of you need think it for a moment!'

This was a long speech for Ma and I could tell she wasn't aiming to budge from her position. 'Suppose she take the baby with her,' Pa suggested, soothing like. 'Then you could get on with what all you need to be doing.'

I chipped in, 'Yes, Ma, I'll take Davy out and give him some fresh air.'

Ma felt that she was being got round, but as so often when my father and I stood together, she did not quite see her way clear to opposing the both of us. She said,

'Well, I will allow there is some sense in that scheme. It would give me a chance to get on a bit, not to mention that child making herself useful. Which is not what I would describe as a common event.'

'Thanks Ma,' I said and scooped up my baby brother before she could change her mind. As I lit out, she called after me,

'And mind you don't drop that baby or lose him or something. Your pa might consider you sharp as a lancet, but from all I know of you, you have no more sense than a grasshopper!'

I put out my tongue and pulled a face at that, but seeing as my back was to her, it did not really signify. I settled Davy into my arms and since he was a biddable child and not given to crying over much, it looked to be an enjoyable morning.

Now for the geography lesson, which perhaps you thought I had forgot! The area we had settled in can be described easily in one word; and that word is 'grass'. Grass before, grass behind, grass on either side, as far as the eye could see, just grass and nothing more. And the land was more or less completely flat. I once visited the county of Lincolnshire in England and it struck me as somewhat similar, which is to say bleak and monotonous. Scattered at wide intervals were soddies similar to our own, from some of which smoke trickled up into the clear blue sky. The overall monotony of grass was also broken here and there by dark rectangles where fields

45

had been ploughed and planted. Some of these had fences round them and this was another bane to ranchers like Anderson. Of which I shall say more later.

The land was not completely flat, it undulated somewhat, particularly by the river where we were. This river, which ran down and joined the Niobrara a few miles away, had carved a wide, shallow valley, so we had to walk a half mile up a very gentle slope before we could view the plains. I never heard tell as to why there were no trees in that part of the country; that's just the way it was.

I must say something here about the way people whom I met spoke. They all had different accents and ways of expressing themselves. Some, like Ikey, had distinctive styles of speech. My mother's accent was different from the women in Zion and so on. I shall not attempt to reproduce those differences here. It would be wearisome and you must just imagine that different people spoke in different styles.

The first house I came to had a nice little garden planted out front, with bright red flowers edging the vegetable beds. I felt shy about knocking on the door, so I just stood there admiring the flowers. The door opened and out came Ikey, the boy who my father had rescued. He smiled and said,

'Hidy!'

'Hallo.'

'I was hoping you'd come by. Ain't nobody much our age in the whole entire valley.'

'How old are you?'

'Gonna be fifteen this July.'

'Reckon I got a year on you then,' I said. 'I was fifteen

November gone.'

He shrugged and then asked, 'Is that your baby?'

I laughed. 'Hell, no. He's my brother.'

'Can I hold him?'

'Don't see why not. Only mind you don't drop him.'

Ikey took my brother in his arms and swayed him backwards and forwards a little, which made Davy gurgle with pleasure. Ikey lifted him up a little, bent his head and kissed the baby on his forehead. I had never seen a boy behave so with a baby and found the novelty interesting.

'You like babies?' I asked.

Ikey shrugged, a little embarrassed. 'I reckon.'

The door to their house opened and a tall black woman came out. She was not as black as Ikey, seemed to me that she might have Indian or white blood in her, because her lips were thinner than a lot of black folk and her nose narrow and straight. She chided Ikey for not inviting me into the house and we all went inside. Ikey, his mother and step-pa had been living there for almost a year and it was a cosy little place. Instead of bare earth, they had a proper floor made of boards, and glass windows. There were two pictures on the walls too, coloured prints of Jesus and his disciples.

To save time, I will describe the composition of Ikey's family as I later discovered it to be. Ikey and his ma had been slaves in one of the Southern states, I don't recollect which one off hand. Although now I think on it, Georgia comes to mind. Leastways, I heard some mention of Savannah from somebody in connection with their life before the war. Ikey was only four or five when the war ended. The man he called Pa was from the north. He was a freed man who had fought in the Federal army, and after the fighting he'd met and fallen in love with Ikey's mother. They had moved from place to place in the North, until, like my father, Ikey's step-pa had taken advantage of the Homesteader's Act, which gave that one hundred and sixty acres to those men who had served in the Union forces. Although he had been in a coloured regiment, I gathered later that he and my pa had fought at some of the same battles, although they had not met until we moved to Nebraska.

Ikey's step-pa was not present in the house, being about some business in the agricultural line. His wife, though, bade me be seated and offered me coffee, a drink I seldom had at home. They had a table, at which I sat. It was old, but very clean and scrubbed, just like everything else I could see. Ikey's ma asked me about my family and so on. She referred to Ikey always by his correct name, which was Isaac.

'Tell me, Miss Cade, how do you find our corner of the plains?'

I might also point out something which I noticed about Ikey's family. When I met Al, his step-pa, he just called me Maybelle right from the start, the way any adult would. Ikey's mother though, she would at first address me as 'Miss Cade'. To begin with I was flattered by this, thinking that it made me sound like a grown-up person, but later I realized that it was an act of deference on her part, talking to white folks on equal terms didn't come easy to her and she was liable to fall back into the forms of speech from her days as a slave. However often I would tell her to call me just plain Maybelle, she would smile and the most familiarity she would permit herself was to call me 'Miss Maybelle'.

'I like it just fine round here,' I told Ikey's ma politely. 'Mind, I have not really had much chance to see the sights, because we have been working so hard.'

'Why don't you and Isaac go for a walk now and he might show you what is to be seen near here? Not that there is much, really.'

Ikey was still holding the baby and I looked a little dubious, because it was a sunny day and I did not want little Davy to get too hot. Ikey's ma seemed to divine what was in my mind, because she said, 'Go along now and leave that child with me. I have tended many children; he will come to no harm with me.'

We did not need further encouragement and at once left the house. I have to say that it did not occur to me for a moment that this might be putting Ikey's mother to any sort of inconvenience, that she might have things with which she should be getting on and which would be hindered by having to look after my brother. But there, that is young people all over, selfish and not ever thinking of others.

Although here and there were fences, made chiefly of barbed wire, it was possible to walk round such enclosed areas and just stroll right across the prairie. All these hundred and sixty acre farms were crammed side by side, with no free land in between, but most of the place was not under cultivation yet and there were no fences marking off clearly where one man's property ended and another's began. The unwritten rule was that you could cross a man's land, providing always that you caused no damage, like riding over seeds and suchlike.

Anyways, me and Ikey walked along like the two foolish young children we were, chatting and getting to know each other. Our hands brushed together and then, without either of us thinking anything of it, we clasped hands together, like children on a school outing. We were happy and smiling, both perhaps feeling that we had found somebody who would make a good friend and companion.

We were walking in this fashion when three horsemen rode up on us. Two were unknown to me, but the third was Anderson's foreman who, as I later learned, went by the name of Georgia Jack, coming as he did from that state. This was the man who had ridden up with his boss, hunting for Ikey, on the day we finished our house. There were apparently three other men called Jack among Anderson's employees: Old Jack, Young Jack and Six-Fingered Jack. So it made sense for each Jack to have a word or two attached to his name so as to distinguish him from the others.

Although I had not then known his name, I recognized this Georgia Jack from the incident on the day we completed our house. He looked just as mean as I remembered. Soon as Ikey saw who was coming he tried to relinquish his grasp upon my hand, but I would not let him. The three men rode right up to us, blocking our way. Georgia Jack looked at us with no friendly eye, not failing to notice our clasped hands.

'Where I come from, we got names for girls as goes with black men,' he told us.

'Well, where I come from, folk generally tend to their own affairs.' I replied.

'You have an awful big mouth on you. Comes from having a father who is such a talkative and awkward bastard maybe.'

I bit back the first childish retort that came to mind and after a space observed cooly, 'You're mighty talkative yourself today. You didn't have so much to say when my father drew down on you with his shotgun.'

I knew at once that this hit home because I saw his knuckles whiten where he held the reins. Also, the other two men exchanged glances; they evidently knew something of the story. Georgia Jack saw their shared looks and I could tell that he was really riled up.

'Your father's a dirty whoreson,' he snapped, like we were in the playground cussing each other's folks. 'He's a dirty whoreson and I'd shoot him soon's look at him if'n he cross my way again.'

'Why're you telling me?' I enquired innocently. 'Why don't you go and tell him?'

He turned his attention to Ikey. 'Let me catch you troubling any o' my steers again, you damned black coon, and I'll finish you and your family once for all!'

Having said this he jabbed his spurs viciously into his horse's flanks and if I hadn't grabbed Ikey's arm and jerked him to one side, I believe he would have ridden us both down. He went off at a brisk canter. The other two fellows seemed more amused than angered at this exchange. I guess it was not every day that they saw someone taunt their boss in this way. They seemed to find it a novel and entertaining experience to see him baited in this wise. One of them half smiled at me and touched his hat brim before trotting off after Georgia Jack at a leisurely pace.

When they had gone Ikey sat down on the grass. He looked shaky and could not bring himself to speak for a minute or so. At length, he said, 'Maybelle, what in the *hell* you think you're doing fooling with that killer? Are you outa your mind?'

I shrugged. 'I ain't afeared of him. I reckon my pa could take him any time.'

'Lord God, Maybelle, ain't we got enough troubles already? You are one crazy girl.'

We walked back to his house, where I met for the first time with Ikey's step-pa, Al. Al was a huge man. He was one of those men who were so big that they did not feel the need to throw their weight around and show off. Looking at him you could tell that he was more than capable of taking on most any comer and still coming out on top. Incidentally, here is another thing which I have observed in the world. The bigger or stronger the man, the less need he has to assert himself boastfully and bully others. The opposite is of course also true. I might mention here in passing that when not in the saddle, which was rare, Georgia Jack stood only an inch or so taller than me. You got to wonder if this lack of size might perhaps have given him what I have since heard called an 'inferiority complex'!

When we got to Ikey's house, Al was cleaning the plough. Ikey gave him a colourful and somewhat exaggerated account of our meeting with Georgia Jack. While his stepson was telling the story, Al eyed me thoughtfully and not, as I thought, in any friendly fashion. Looking back over all these years, I can explain now what I would never have guessed at the time. Grateful as he was to my father for rescuing Ikey from a beating or worse at the hands of Anderson and his foreman, Al had sized me up pretty well as a flighty and mischievous young piece of goods, liable to bring only trouble to him and his family. Again, with the passage of all those years since then, I may as well admit that he was not far wrong in his estimation of things.

Look at matters from Al's point of view and you will see what I mean by all the above. Here his wife's son is, only a couple of days earlier having nearly got himself lynched and now this bold young girl fetches up and takes him out walking, only to goad and insult the very man who was so recently after killing his stepson! This is not a good beginning, but there is also the colour thing. I do not think it sat well with Al to return to his home and find his wife nursing a white baby, like she might have done back on some Southern plantation. Maybe it seemed to him that some white girl turns up here and starts treating his own wife like a Mammy. Then again, not everybody was likely to take kindly to the sight of a black boy strolling around with a white girl. This too was the sort of thing to inflame tensions in the neighbourhood and inflaming tensions was the very thing that Al was anxious to avoid just at that juncture.

Be that as it may, when Ikey had finished his tale Al advised him to go and help his ma. He then asked me to wait for a moment and went into his house, returning with my baby brother. Truth to tell, I had forgot all about

Davy by that time and if Al had not reminded me, I might easily have returned to my home without him. When I had Davy in my arms and there was just the two of us, Al gave me his views and opinions on the matter and they were none too flattering to me.

'It is my opinion, Maybelle, that you would have done better to remain silent when you was accosted by those three men,' Al told me bluntly. His wife might be calling me 'Miss Cade' or 'Miss Maybelle', but there was none of that with Al. He simply treated me as he would any child, black or white. 'There is, as I am sure you have heard, plenty of trouble in this place, without your going out to create more.'

'I didn't start it.'

'It is not a question of who starts things. This is not the schoolyard and I am not a teacher neither. I say that there is enough trouble and nobody will thank you for making more. Who started what is not at issue, you did not need to speak so to that man.'

Something about the way he spoke put me in mind of my father. There was that same straightforward way of saying what he thought needed to be said. I did not much take to what he was saying, but I realized at the back of my mind that he would speak in just the same direct way even if he were talking to the President of the USA. Feeling perhaps that he had been a mite harsh in his words, Al smiled at me and said, 'This does not mean that we are not going to be friends, Maybelle, only that I would be mighty obliged to you not to lead that boy in harm's way. Your father is a right smart man and he and I have spoken at some length. I am sure that if you ask him, he will tell you the same thing.'

Of this I had not the slightest doubt, and had already decided privately to keep the day's events to my own self. I did not want my father to know that as soon as I was out of his sight I was getting into mischief. Al looked at me thoughtfully, as if trying to gauge just how troublesome I was likely to prove as a near neighbour. Then he smiled again. 'Your father and me have it in mind to conduct a little business together in the next few days and so I think that we shall meet again before too long.' He nodded to me in a friendly enough way and then went back into his house, leaving me to walk home.

CHAPTER 5

After my little run in with Georgia Jack I didn't see Ikey or his step-pa for a few days. There was plenty of work to do round the place, both in the house and the fields. For example, when my father first ploughed up a field, the result was as I have described, long cables of earth. Well, I had sometimes to chop up those long strips of earth with a spade. Then I had to walk up and down collecting large stones and setting them out of the way. It was hard work and I used to get out of it whenever the opportunity presented itself.

I am not about to torment you with a long and wordy description of farming on the great plains in the days before your own grandparents were likely born, but I will say that it was an arduous business. Much has been made of the pioneers of that time, but I am here to tell you now that it was no sort of fun at the time, nor romantic either. It was just damned hard work with little reward.

I have nigh on told you all about my personal life as a homesteader, it is now time to talk about what was going on in the district in a wider sense. Much of this, I only found out later. I had heard a few things though, and observed one or two more myself. Cattle driven over planted fields, fences torn up at night, things of that nature. Now this might sound trifling enough, but when you are a subsistence farmer, grubbing a living from the soil in this way, a fence being torn down can be a major disaster. Instead of getting on with sowing and ploughing, you have instead to waste a day repairing a fence. Similarly, damaging crops is more than a slight nuisance. Most of the men there had brought seed with them to plant. If crops were damaged and needed to be replanted, it might mean buying seed in town. The merchants there knew a sellers' market when they saw it and few of the settlers had much in the way of cash money. This sort of thing could make the difference between a man just getting by, grubbing a living, and his family being on the edge of starvation.

One way of getting out of working in the field was by offering to go to town and bring back any provisions we might need. My father was pleased when I volunteered to do this, but my mother looked at me as though she was quite aware that I was trying to wriggle out of doing any proper work. Two or three days after I had spoken to Al, I found myself deputed to visit Zion with a view to purchasing a bag of meal. I had not told my mother or father anything at all about the unfortunate scene with Anderson's foreman and had congratulated myself on having avoided an unpleasant interview with my father. There were many things about which he would turn a blind eye if he observed one or the other of them in me, but discourteous behaviour was not among them. He would not be happy to hear that I had been sassing a grown-up and bringing him into the conversation into the bargain.

I had been helping my mother in the morning by washing Davy and taking the wares down to the stream to clean them properly. It must have been eleven o'clock or so, with the sun almost at its zenith, when I set off towards town. It was a beautiful day and I did not take any particular hurry, because of course as soon as I got back there would be something else found for me to do.

The town made a change from seeing nothing but grass but, truth to tell, it was not a marvellously interesting place. Folks were busy with their own affairs and although they were polite enough, nodding and saying 'Good morning', you got the feeling that there was an undercurrent of unease, like they were nervous of something unexpected happening. That morning I saw what sort of thing they were worried about.

Something which I have noticed about violence between men is that it very often happens suddenly, with no prior warning at all. Some men will be talking peaceably in a bar room and then one will take exception to a fancied slight and he will without signalling in any wise his intentions, turn over a table and begin slugging it out with the others. I have seen a heap of violence in my time and it is the unpredictable and seemingly random nature of it that I have always found disturbing.

After buying the meal from the provisions store, I dawdled back along the main street. Ahead of me was a man carrying a new spade that he looked to have recently acquired, and coming towards us were three men. By their spurs and other rigging, I figured these three for cowhands. I was only about ten feet or so behind the man with the spade, whom I took to be a homesteader. He moved aside for the three men and as soon as they had passed him, walking towards me, one of them whirled round and accosted the man they had just passed, saying angrily, 'Say what, you son of a bitch?'

Now I was close enough to have heard if the man being challenged had actually spoken. I would take oath that he had said nothing and indeed, he appeared surprised to be called to in this way. 'Who, me?' he asked, mildly enough.

'Yes you, you cow's son!' said the man who had first spoken and, with no further ado, he launched himself at the bewildered man with a ferocity which was awful to watch. Once he had knocked the fellow to the ground, the two other men joined in, kicking and leaning over to throw punches at his face. The solid thunk of fists and boots was sickening to hear and it went on for perhaps a minute or two. I stood aghast, scarcely believing what I was seeing. As if at a signal, the three men stopped their assault and walked casually away from the figure lying in the dust.

I went over to him to see if I could help, but after groaning and swearing a little, he stood up and shook the dust off his clothes. Then he did something which disgusted me. He grimaced a little, pulled his mouth into a strange pucker and then spat out a mouthful of blood, into which was mixed a gleaming white tooth. He picked up his spade and, still ignoring me, continued on his way. The really strange thing was that nobody seemed at all surprised or put out by this violent attack. You might think that folk would come rushing out to help or call for the men who were beating him to desist, but you would be wrong. Nobody even appeared to notice the incident. Even the victim himself did not seem surprised by what had occurred.

This was something of a novelty in my hitherto sheltered existence and I could not wait to get home to tell my mother and father about what I had seen. I trotted homewards at a brisk pace, only to slow down considerably when I neared our home and saw my father standing by the door talking to Al. My heart sank at once. I could guess easily enough how this situation was likely to develop. Nothing remains hidden for ever in this world and, as it says in Scripture, 'What today you whisper in a darkened room, will tomorrow be shouted from the very rooftops'. Which is to say that it seemed likely to me that Al would have told my father all that he knew of my dealings with the foreman. So it proved.

I will also say here that Pa had an almost supernatural knack of knowing or discovering if I had been up to any kind of mischief. The keener I was on concealing it from him, the more likely it was to come to light. I could conceal things at times from Ma, but from my father, never.

As I came nigh to the house, my father indicated that he wished to have some words with me. I could tell by the look on his face that this was not to be in the nature of a pleasant interview.

'Maybelle, our neighbour here tells me that you have been disputing in what sounds to me like a saucy manner with a grown-up person. Is this so?'

'It's not what it sounds like, Pa. He was rude to me.'

'That has no bearing on the case. I am not best pleased to hear of this, Maybelle. I also hear where you have been bragging about what you perceive as my prowess, again with this same person. Is this also true?'

I just nodded. Pa was usually so friendly and easy with me and now here he was upbraiding me in front of a stranger. I could feel my cheeks burning and for a moment, I felt as though I hated Al. I stood silently, waiting for my father to dismiss me and hoping that he had finished, but this was not so.

'Speaking in this way to others is not what I have raised you to, Maybelle. I would have looked for you to remain silent and then bring the matter to my attention. Worse still, is where you have tried to deceive me, hoping that I would not hear what had chanced. I am right displeased with you. Go to your mother now and see if she has any chores to occupy you. We will speak further on this.'

I went into the house almost in tears. I could not remember a time when my father had been so stern with me, and what made it worse was that he had spoken like this in front of somebody else. It was only years later, when I had children of my own, that I understood that he was terrified out of his wits on my behalf and it was this which caused him to speak so harshly. You know how it is when your small child runs into the road and nearly gets knocked down by an automobile? You are so frightened that you do not at first cuddle the child, but instead deliver a slap. This was how it was with Pa when he found that I had been provoking a notorious killer. He saw the danger that I had been in and was mindful of what could have happened to me.

I said to my ma, 'P-pa says t-to ask if you have any ch-chores for me.' I could hardly get out the words, I was feeling that mortified about being scolded so.

'So that is the way of it,' remarked my mother. 'I have heard somewhat of this business and since your father has seen fit to rebuke you, I have nothing further to say of the matter. Come here.' I went to her and she opened her arms and drew me to her, whereupon I began weeping. She comforted me as though I were a small child, before wiping my eyes and getting me to blow my nose.

'Maybelle, things are not as we could wish them to be. There is a heap of trouble here and my private feeling is that we would be better to be back in Pittsburgh. That is all I have to say on that subject. You must try to help and not give your father fresh cause for concern. I think that you are old enough to understand this; you are no longer a little girl.'

I nodded without saying anything. My mother asked me to fetch some water from the stream. I went there and filled the pot. When I turned to take it back to the house, I found Al standing there, watching me. I could not meet his eyes, I was so shamed at the thought of his seeing and hearing of my disgrace. He came up to me and said,

'Are you vexed with me, Maybelle, for telling your pa about what happened?'

I bridled a little and then said quietly, 'I guess a bit.'

'I will tell you how things stand and then you can judge me as you see fit. There are things going on around here which could mean life or death for some of us. Anything which tends towards making matters worse needlessly is to be avoided. Your father is a deep thinker and will not speak or act until he has weighed up everything. I too think hard on all that I say and do. It need only one thoughtless or, as it might be, careless word to provide the spark which will set off the powderkeg. For this reason we would all do well to set a watch upon our words.'

Al looked at me for a space and then stretched out his hand. 'So are we friends, Maybelle?'

'Yes, sir.' I shook his hand and we walked back to where my father stood. He still looked serious, but had I think been glad to see me and Al shake hands.

After Al had gone home we ate, and I told my mother and father about the beating which I had seen administered to the man in Zion. Pa looked thoughtful. When we had eaten, he said to me, 'Maybelle, perhaps you would favour me with your company for a spell?' This sounded less like a request than it did an order. We walked in silence to where he had left the plough and the hobbled oxen. When we got there, he looked at me and laid his hand on my shoulder. 'You think that I was hard on you earlier and that is so. I have my reasons for it.' He motioned that we should sit on the ground together.

'I am going to tell you how things stand, Maybelle Louise. It is not in reason that I should ask you to obey blindly any instruction of mine and so I will impress upon you the importance of what I say by being plain about it.'

I hardly knew what to make of this, but I think that my father was, as well as trying to make up with me, using me as what is known as a sounding board, to get clear in his own mind what he was about.

'I have not spoken overmuch to either you or your mother of what passed in the war. It was a bloody business and the less said about it the better. Most of those who took part were like me, just ordinary soldiers who did what they felt they should do. Sometimes we killed and at other times we got killed ourselves. Most soldiers have no relish for killing, it is a matter of kill or be killed. It is altogether a beastly affair.'

Pa looked drawn and old while he talked about this and I could see why he did not like to revisit those memories. I leaned my head on his shoulder and he smiled at me, ruffling my hair. I was so glad that we were not at outs any more. He continued to tell me what was on his mind.

'Most soldiers feel like I did about killing. I can meet Confederate soldiers now and get along with them just fine, we neither of us want to hold any hard feelings about what happened in the war. Howsoever, there are some in every war who do not feel that way. These are men who enjoy killing and looting. They walk upright like men, but they have souls like wild beasts. Such a one is Anderson's foreman, him they call Jack.'

'You've only known him for a few days, Pa. How can you be so sure about him?'

My father then astonished me by saying, 'I have known

this man longer than a few days. I was familiar with him better than ten years ago, back about 1864. I did not know it was he until I was talking now to Al. It is the same man, there is no shadow of a doubt.'

'Well, who is he? How'd you know him?'

'Have you heard tell of a man called Quantrill?'

'I do not recollect the name. Who is he?'

'He was a Confederate soldier during the war. He led a band of what are called by some "bandits". He and his men killed many innocent people. At one town, a place called Lawrence, they killed every male person, ranging from fourteen-year-old boys to old men of ninety. He was a wicked man. I was there in Kentucky when he was killed.'

I was hearing more of my father's life in the war than he had ever before vouchsafed to me. I also suspected that he had not shared these memories with my mother.

'If he's dead, what has he to do with this here problem?'

'I will explain. Quantrill was right close to two men. One was a man who was half-Cherokee, what some would call a half-breed. His name was Joel Mayes and he hailed from Bartow County, Georgia. It was he who taught Quantrill about guerrilla tactics and ambushes. Quantrill's right-hand man was called Anderson, he was known as 'Bloody Bill' Anderson. Joel Mayes had a younger brother called Jack. He rode with Quantrill until the end and he was one of the worst blackguards that ever lived.'

I was beginning to see where this might be leading, and carried on listening without interrupting.

'Tell me,' said my father, 'did you notice anything special about him they call Georgia Jack?'

I considered this question for a space, then replied, 'He is very brown. I have not often seen a white man with such a complexion.'

'It is because he is part-Indian, just like his brother Joel,' said my father. 'I thought that I had seen this fellow before when he and his boss visited us. Judging from how he stared at me, I wonder if he felt the same. Talking to Al now, I find that this is the same man who was riding with Quantrill when we captured him. I am of the opinion also that this Anderson who is such an important man in these parts is a relative of "Bloody Bill" Anderson. It all fits in together. And now I tell you, Maybelle, that that man whom you were so foolish as to bandy words with so lightly, would kill you or me without thinking twice on the matter. Do you now see why I spoke so to you, apart from any other reason? You are my child and I would not wish you to breathe the same air as Jack Mayes, let alone get crosswise to him.'

After Pa said all this to me we sat there for a time without saying nothing. I could see that my father had trusted me with a deal of information, more than he had ever done before. I also began to see why he and our neighbour did not want me aggravating the situation by running off at the mouth to this dangerous man. We sat in companionable silence for a minute or so, before my father touched my hair lightly and said, 'I do not wish you to talk of this to anybody, not even your Ma. I will do what is needful to tackle this affair, but there is nothing to be gained from talking about it beforehand like. Just let it set and I will think on what must be done. And keep your own counsel, should you meet this man again.'

My father stood up and so did I. He kissed me on the forehead and then looked doubtful as to whether he had made himself sufficiently clear. 'Maybelle,' he said, 'I can tell you without boasting that I am not a cowardly man. I have killed men and would do so again if need arose. Still and all, I tell you plainly that this Jack Mayes is one I would be very cautious about going up against. I have both heard of his actions during the war and I have also seen the consequences. It is enough for you to know that he has killed women and children both, with no hesitation. That you should stand in front of such a man with your saucy ways fills me with dread. Do not let it occur again, for my sake, if not your own.' He then dispatched me homewards to help my mother around the house, while he continued with the ploughing.

CHAPTER 6

Now I am thinking that anybody reading this account will be thinking to theyselves, 'Golly, events surely coming thick and fast in such a short space of time! Seems like nobody has time to draw breath before the next episode is upon them.' The reason for this is not hard to divine. We had arrived in the area at what you might call the climax of the affair. In other words, tensions had been rising and running high for the best part of a year and things were now entering what a chess player would call the end game. Even if we had not settled there, I believe that there would have been bloodletting and violence and either the big rancher or the little farmers would then have come out on top. That at least is the way I see things now, at a distance of some decades.

After he heard about my foolish words with Jack Mayes, my father took good care that I should not have too much leisure for roaming the plains and putting myself in danger. One way and another, he and my mother made sure that I had plenty to occupy my day-light hours. Perhaps a week after the conversation which

I have related above, Pa sent me off with a spade to break up some of the furrows that he had ploughed earlier in the day. Also with a big basket so that I could gather up any stones and move them to the side of the field. After perhaps an hour of this endeavour, I came back to the house for a drink, only to find my father and Al sitting on the ground, smoking their pipes and talking quietly.

Now my father did not in general take kindly to my interrupting adult conversations. When talking to Al, he struck me as particularly keen that I should not involve myself in the discussion. Most of their talk took place out of earshot. I suspect now that my father did not want his talkative fifteen-year-old daughter hearing of any private arrangements or secret plans that he and Al might be hatching. Who can blame him? Not me! Still, there was nothing to be lost by the attempt and so I smiled in what I thought was a winning way at Al and then sat down next to Pa, leaning against him. He gave me a look, as though to say, *Don't try your coaxing ways with me, miss, I know you too well!* Howsoever, he did not send me about my business, which I viewed in the nature of a triumph.

Al glanced at me and then I suppose thought that if my father did not mind my hearing, then it was not his place to object. He continued what he had evidently been saying before I sat down.

'The plain fact is, Ebenezer, that matters are coming to a head, whether or no we want them to. If we don't stand firm, we might as well just pack up and leave right now.' My father said nothing for a space. He just sat and smoked. After a few moments' thought, he spoke.

'I done enough fighting in the war, Al. I reckon you

did as well.'

'It ain't a matter of fighting. It is simply this: are we fixing to stay or are we going to leave?'

Again, my father sat without speaking.

'What have you in mind, Al?' he asked at length.

'Same as you, I reckon. Nobody talking about fighting, Ebenezer. You are right, I had my fill of all that in the war, same as you. I'm talking about keeping what's ours, safe.'

'I will not deny,' said my father slowly, 'that I have been thinking about a vigilance committee of our own, to keep order in our part of the valley. What you are talking about though is something different. You think it will come down to a shooting match and that we must be prepared for some species of war.'

Al shrugged. 'It amounts to the same thing, call it what you will. We need to organize ourselves, so that if one of us is troubled, all the other homesteaders come to his aid. It ain't us damaging folk's property. I had another fence tore down last night.'

'It would take some organizing,' my father said at last. 'People would need to be told what to do and when. Is that the sort of responsibility that you want, Al? I am here to tell you, this will be a thankless task. Anderson and his cowboys will be targeting you as soon as you begin and then on the other side, all the other homesteaders would blame you for any trouble that ensued. A mighty thankless task, like I say.'

Al laughed, a long, rich belly-laugh of genuine amusement. 'They ain't likely to take instructions from a black man! They would be wanting somebody who knows how to organize things and tell men what to do. An officer.'

My father stirred uneasily and looked down at me. 'Maybelle,' he said, 'go and help your ma.' Then he stood up and said to Al, 'We will not talk further of this matter here. Let's walk off a pace or two and I will tell you what I think on it.' Which was my father's way of saying, *Landsakes Al, don't let that daughter of mine know what's what. She'll make sure to spread the news far and wide!*

A few days later my father announced at dinner that that night he would be going out for a spell with some of the other men who had settled in the valley. 'Going out, Ebenezer?' enquired my mother in a puzzled fashion. 'Why, where are you going? Surely you are not aiming to visit the saloon or something?'

My father smiled at this. I also smiled and ducked my head, but a mite to late to avoid my mother seeing. The idea of my father supping whiskey in a saloon was just too funny. 'And perhaps you would care to tell me why that child is smiling, as well? It seems to me that some more plans have been made here to which I have not been a party. Only the baby is less well informed than me about what goes on in this family!'

'Don't take on,' said my father comfortably. 'I am just going to be discussing farming matters with them and making plans. The saloon does not enter into the scheme. As to Maybelle laughing, well it seems to me she is still a bit too light-hearted and carefree for her own good. I am sure that you will be able to find some chores to occupy her gainfully?'

I guessed of course that my father had agreed to set up this vigilance committee and I also was pretty sure that he would be leading it. After all, he had been an officer and it was plain to all who met him that he was a God-fearing and trustworthy man. Another thing about him was that it was obvious that he did not really seek power and responsibility. It had to be thrust upon him, as you might say. He would only take on duties if he felt it was for other people's good. I have to say that this type was rare enough then and has grown a sight rarer since! I am not just saying that because he was my father; it is just the kind of man he was. Strange that those men who seek power and leadership are often the ones least suited to the job, while the men who genuinely don't want power are the very ones best able to exercise it. Well, that's how it is in this world.

I should now say a few words about the wider aspects of our lives as homesteaders. I have already explained that the big ranchers were getting annoyed because the open range no longer belonged to them. Not that it had ever technically done so, but for many years the land there had just been available for anybody to use as they saw fit. I have also, I think, said that most people who moved into the plains wanted to set up near a ready source of water such as a river or stream. For those running large herds of cattle, finding themselves cut off from such access to water was one cause of irritation. Another was the fences, which were springing up all over the place. You have to remember that barbed wire had just been invented a few years previously and it revolutionised farming and changed the face of the land almost at once. Before this useful stuff came along, you needed a whole heap of wood to build any sort of fence or barrier. This in itself was a problem when you lived in an area like ours, which had no trees anywhere. Also, no sort of wooden fence is likely to keep large animals in or out effectively. With barbed wire, you just need a few strong stakes driven into the ground and then you string the wire from one post to the next. Hey presto, you have a fence that is strong and will keep farm animals in or out according to your wishes. Just what you want when running a farm. From the point of view of the ranchers, this was an absolute nightmare.

As I think I have said, the general rule was that you could cross a man's land as long as you did so peaceably without causing any harm. Driving a few hundred head of cattle across his fields was apt to be something else again, though. I believe that some of these cowboys would anyway have done this: let their herds cross farmed land, but with fences of barbed wire being erected around fields, it was easier and quicker just to go round them. Here then is where the problem becomes serious. Suppose you take your cattle round one field enclosed by barbed wire, only then to encounter another and another. Pretty soon, the range is split up like this and you cannot pasture and water any cattle at all.

To be fair to the ranchers, before us people had showed up they had unlimited grassland to graze their herds on, plenty of water, no restrictions at all in fact. You can see where they might get a bit peeved about finding the land covered in barbed wire fences and ploughed fields, having to travel twenty miles to get to the river-bank and suchlike. All because the government had took it into they heads to give away the land to a heap of no account dirt farmers! Yes, I can see where they surely felt aggrieved about the matter.

After my pa had gone off that evening, my mother kept me busy with various odd jobs. Most of these were of the make-work variety; piddling little things that didn't really need doing, but were calculated to keep me occupied and out of mischief. Out of the blue, my mother asked me, 'What is it your pa is up to, Maybelle?' I did not know what to reply to this and so said nothing.

'Do not think for a moment,' said my mother, 'that I am not aware that your father is about something. I also have a strong idea that you know somewhat of the matter. So I will ask you again, what is he doing?'

'I think he and the other men are just arranging to watch after each other's interests, Ma,' I told her. 'So that if one family has trouble then the others will come and help.'

She looked at me for a second or two without speaking, then said, 'What sort of trouble might we be talking of here, Maybelle? Is he starting up some band of armed men? It is not so long since we have finished with a civil war. I do not much take to the idea of being involved in another such.'

'Oh, Ma, it's nothing like that. I think they just worry that Anderson and his men are getting a bit contentious and Pa and his friends are wanting to discourage them a little.'

My mother said nothing more and we sat there in a friendly fashion for a space, which was not common for us at that time in my life. At last she said, 'I hope that coming out West like this has not been a mistake.

Pittsburgh was mighty dirty and noisy, but when you grow a little older you will realize that noise and dirt are not the worst things in this life, no, not by a long measure.'

My father did not return until late that night. Ma and me were still setting up by the light of the oil lamp, talking in an amiable way about this, that and nothing in particular. Like I say, this was not common at that stage in my life and I think we both relished the occasion for that reason. Pa looked tired and somewhat more serious than usual, which was saying something, because he was not, even at the best of times, what you could call a light-hearted and vivacious type of man. He appeared pleased to find his wife and daughter waiting up for him and he kissed us both in greeting. Then he sat down and addressed us thus:

'Well, I dare say that you will both have formed some idea of my purpose in going out to meet with our neighbours tonight. It was to discuss the setting up of a combination to protect our interests and prevent any encroachments upon our liberty. This has been done and we have agreed that we will help each other in the future and that one man's problems will be met with the assistance of all.'

'You make this sound like some benevolent society,' observed my mother. 'In what form will this aid be distributed, Ebenezer? Are you going to be providing for the widow and orphan, according to the Bible? If so, then this enterprise is worthy of you.'

'I do not think, Martha, that this should be a cause for levity,' he reproved her.

'I am sorry that you should think that I find this in the

slightest amusing. I do not. Tell me straight out what you are about and we will see then whether this is a thing to laugh about.'

Pa said nothing for a bit. Then at length he said, 'You are right. I should come out and tell you just what we purpose. It is a vigilance committee and I have been chosen to lead it.'

It was obvious to both me and my father that Ma did not at all take to this notion. She pursed her lips and then spoke again. 'Since this seems to be an evening for plain speaking, then I too will say my piece. I do not like any of this. Why are you the leader of this band? You must know that in such a case, the person who leads these things is the target of anger by the lawless and also that those he leads will generally turn out to be ungrateful, blaming him for any misfortune which results. Why have you allowed yourself to be put in such a false position? Could you not have refused?'

'If a man is in the right, Martha, then he has no business refusing a position of this sort. It would be like a soldier deserting his post or a man called to jury service who dodged like a fox to evade his duty. I have been your husband these sixteen years, you know the man I am.'

My mother softened a little and looked sadly at Pa. 'Yes, Ebenezer, I know the man you are and that is why I married you. You have not changed and for that I am thankful. Still, I wish this had not taken place. I fear for you.'

There was little to be said after that and so we slept.

CHAPTER 7

Within a week, my father had organized the homestead-ers around Zion into a loose federation. With one or two exceptions – men who hoped to avoid trouble by keeping their heads down – it had been agreed that every-body would stick together against any encroachment from Anderson. My father was hoping to create some sort of community spirit among the farmers and thought that this might extend beyond mere defence and cause them to help each other out in other areas as well. He explained much of this to me while we worked together.

'How it is, Maybelle, is that there is not room enough now for Anderson and his herds as well us our little farms. One or the other maybe, but not both. That is not, though, the whole story. I hope that by riding patrol together and guarding each others' fields, that the men in this valley will begin to think like friends and fellow strugglers. Not like each is alone and fighting against the world, but that we all have friends we can call on in need.'

'So what'll happen, Pa?'

'You mean Anderson and his bullies? I guess that he will try and make a move on some of us, one at a time.'

'Make a move? What sort of move?'

My father stopped cleaning the plough and stood up, looking down to the river. He did not say anything for a minute or so. Then he said, 'I think, Maybelle, that he will try and pick a quarrel with somebody and maybe start a fight. Then, if he can do the man so that he and his family move off the land, he will get one of his boys to stake claim to it. If he can do that with a half-dozen of the families near here, then those remaining will probably feel scared and try their luck elsewhere.'

'So what are you aiming to do, Pa?'

He looked back in the direction of our house. 'Since there is no lawman within a few days' ride, we will take over the job ourselves, at least around here. Up to this point Anderson has had pretty much of a free hand. Our vigilance committee will now keep order on this part of the range and not his cowboys.'

I think that my father was really just thinking out loud. Talking to me in this wise gave him a chance to set his thoughts in order. I said, 'But Pa, what about Anderson's vigilance committee? They hung that man we saw on the way here, didn't they?'

'Well then, perhaps it will come to this, Maybelle: we might have to see whose will is the stronger. We have the land and our homes are here. Anderson's boys are working for pay. I'm thinking that people fight harder for their family and homes than they will for money. We shall see what we shall see.'

My father had organized the undertaking along military

lines, the idea being that at night there should be patrols criss-crossing the territory covered by the various farms. Two men riding together could hardly hope to cover the whole area in this way, but once the word got out that this was happening every night, this should in itself be enough to deter some of the minor villainy from taking place.

One of the more pleasurable and exciting consequences of all that was taking place was that my father took it into his head to teach me how to shoot and generally handle firearms. I will say at this point that I think my father sometimes wished that he had a son old enough to work with him and stand in for him in his absence. Because of this lack, from time to time he fell back upon me and treated me more like a boy than a girl. This was irksome to my Ma, as it had the effect of bringing me closer to my father and correspondingly further from her.

Since agreeing to organize the patrols, which would, it was hoped, protect our interests, I noticed that my father had taken to wearing a gun while he worked round the place. I had seen our old fowling piece many times, even when we lived in Pittsburgh, but I had not known that he even owned a pistol. He told me that it was an old cap and ball revolver from when he was in the army. It did not take cartridges, but had to be loaded with a flask of powder and used the same little copper percussion caps as the shotgun. Al too always had a gun at hand when I saw him.

My mother flat refused to have anything to do with guns and my father thought it advisable that when he was away at least one person in the house knew how to shoot. He and I accordingly went down to the river early one morning with his shotgun. He started right from scratch, showing me how to clean and load it. This was exceedingly interesting for a fifteen-year-old girl: being not only allowed, but encouraged to handle a deadly weapon in this way!

This was a muzzle-loading piece and the way it worked was as follows. First, a charge of powder had to be poured down each barrel. Pa had a powder flask which measured off the right amount, so that was easy enough. Next went a piece of lint which was pushed in with the ramrod. This stopped the gunpowder running out again. Then went an ounce or so of lead shot, which is tiny grains of lead. This was followed by another piece of wadding which was also rammed tight. Then you had to put little copper percussion caps over the nipples which lay beneath the hammers and you were ready to go.

I think that I have already said that this is what is known as a 'single-action' gun, which means that pulling the trigger will not both raise and let fall the hammer, but that each time you fired it, the hammer had first to be raised in position or 'cocked', as it is known.

The first time I fired that thing I did not hold it tight into my shoulder and the recoil left a bruise which was still showing a week later! The second time I kept it hard-pressed against me, but did not allow for the thing bucking up as I fired. The result was that I fired way too high. 'Aim low,' said my father. 'That way, you will take into account the tendency of the piece to kick up when you fire.'

Pa did not want to waste too much powder and shot, but by the end of the morning I could at least load and fire the thing, even if my aim was not that fine. Still, as Pa remarked, it did not much signify, because, in the first place, this was a shotgun, not a sniper's rifle. It would throw a heap of lead in somebody's general direction should the need arise. Secondly, of course, was that the person staring down the barrel of a shotgun does not usually stop to ask hisself questions about how keen a shot the party holding the weapon is. It was to be hoped that the very fact of my being able to handle the thing would in itself be enough to discourage any folk from taking liberties with us when my father was away.

Before he let me have a go with his pistol as well, my father shared with me some more information about the use of shotguns as deadly weapons.

'The point with shotguns, Maybelle, is that they are not accurate above a short distance. With a rifle, you can lie in wait for prey, be it human or animal, and sometimes take it from half a mile or more, but those tactics will not answer with a weapon such as this. You must get right up close. The good point about a weapon of this nature is that any man in his senses is scared to have one aimed at him and will likely do as you say while it is pointing in his direction.'

'How come you use little specks of lead and not one large chunk?'

'That is an excellent question, Maybelle. The answer is this. If you used one big piece of lead from an unrifled barrel like this, it would be very inaccurate and only hit something which it was actually heading at. The lead shot, though, spreads out quickly and after twenty yards will cover perhaps six feet or so. This will kill a rabbit or bird. You do not need to be good at aiming.'

All this made sense to me. While he cleaned the gun, he made some additional remarks upon the nature of this type of weapon.

'Sometimes it can be difficult obtaining lead shot and this again is where the shotgun is a handy weapon, especially under circumstances such as our own. You can load it not only with buckshot, but also grit and small stones. Mind, there is something here to recall and that is this. Accidents happen when out hunting. It is a rare man who does not end up getting a few pieces of buckshot in him if he is in the habit of going out hunting with friends. I have had several mishaps of this sort my own self. Such a wound will generally heal itself. If however you have been using grit, stones and soil in your charge, that will not be so apt to heal cleanly. In fact an injury of that sort nearly always turns bad and the victim is liable to die of the lockjaw or blood poisoning or something in that line.'

I only fired the pistol a half dozen times, because we did not have much in the way of ammunition for it. My father had a mould to make bullets, but he still wished to conserve the small amount of lead which he had. Back at the house, my mother made her views clear to us.

'I cannot think what is in your mind, Ebenezer, to let that child start fooling around with a deadly weapon. She will meddle with your gun one day while you are out and the consequence will be that she will shoot the baby or herself.'

'I do not look for that to happen. Maybelle has sense enough to know not to touch the weapon unless there is need.'

Now here is another of those occasions in my story when events come just at the right time, so neatly fitting together that it is like a stage play or movie or something. We saw a similar thing happen when no sooner had we finished building our house than it was needed to give shelter to Ikey. All I can tell you is that life is sometimes like that, with things slotting into place as neat as in a storybook. So it chanced that within twenty four hours of my father showing me how to handle the shotgun, I had need to take it in my hands and prepare to use it.

I was sound asleep, the night after my pa had instructed me in the use of firearms, sleeping as only a young and healthy person can. Which is to say that nothing common would be likely to rouse me from my slumbers. What woke me was my father shaking my shoulder urgently. I mumbled something in a confused way and as soon as he knew that I was awake, he spoke in a fast, low voice.

'There is some species of trouble, Maybelle. Rouse yourself and stand there by the window-slit.' I did so, groggy with sleep and only the embers of last night's cooking-fire to show me the way. My father handed me the shotgun. 'Take this and have it ready to use. It is loaded and primed, but the hammers are not cocked. Do not cock the piece unless there is a threat. I do not wish to return home and have you discharge this at me. If anybody approaches the house, call a challenge and only cock and fire if there is clear evidence of a mortal threat.

I do not look for it, but wish you to stand guard as a precaution.'

With that he was off into the night. I heard him ride off on Dollar and could only assume that he was riding bareback, as he surely had no time to saddle up the animal.

I have no idea how long I stood there in the almost complete darkness, cradling in my arms my father's fowling piece. I was chilly and at length got properly dressed and then went outside. The night was dark and only the stars looked down upon me from a clear sky. My mother and Davy were still sleeping, so I felt very much alone. I checked the gun as my father had shown me, making sure that there were caps over the nipples. I then sat down outside the soddy, with the weapon pointing out vaguely across the prairie. I had been sitting there for a length of time, perhaps half an hour, possibly longer, when I heard a shot. It sounded to be some distance away, although it is hard to gauge this in open country. I at once stood up and became more alert.

The shot was followed by another and then there was a perfect fusillade of firing, ragged volleys which filled me with terror in case my father were in the midst of this affair. There were one or two more single shots and then silence. I strained my ears and could hear from a long distance the noise of men shouting and then a dog barking. Then there was once again complete silence.

I had no idea what had taken place and was thinking that I might next be called upon to defend our home against a band of armed marauders, when I became aware that a lone rider was trotting towards me from up along the valley. I cocked my piece and raised it to my shoulder. The rider crossed the slight rise of ground and was for a moment silhouetted against the sky. Since it was all but pitch black, I was still unable to determine the identity of the horseman and when he was within about fifty yards of the house, I called out in as strong a voice as I could muster, 'Stand to! I am armed and my piece is cocked. If you advance further, I shall fire.'

From out of the darkness came the voice of my father, saying, 'Put up your weapon, Maybelle. And then uncock it. I do not wish to be slain by my own daughter. Tell me when you have done so.'

I fumbled with the hammers and lowered them both gently over the caps. I then apprised my father that this had been done, upon hearing which he advanced. In the meantime, this shouting had awoken my mother, who lit the oil lamp and came out of the house in her nightgown to find me with a shotgun in my hands. My father rode up at the same moment, causing my mother to say, 'It is just as I said it would be yesterday, the child is out here with a deadly weapon for the Lord knows what purpose in the middle of the night.'

'She is using the thing under my instruction,' said my father. 'She has not taken up arms under her own intentions, but is following orders.'

'Lordy, if this don't beat all! You are aiming to instruct her in the use of firearms and target shooting in the middle of the night? Where is the sense in that?'

It took some while to explain matters to my mother and by this time dawn was breaking and there was little purpose in retiring to bed again. My father told us what had happened. He was a light sleeper and had been woken by the sound of a shot. It was at this point that he had roused me and set me to stand guard. When he rode off, he had heard voices and come upon a scene of some confusion. The two men who were riding patrol that night had been shot at by some unknown person and had then come across a lone figure on foot. They had come close to shooting this person, who actually turned out to be a fellow farmer who, being restless and unable to sleep, had taken it into his head to go for a constitutional in the dark. I thought then and still believe it to be the case that at such a time of heightened fear and alarm, this was a foolhardy action on his part.

It had been agreed that those on patrol should fire a shot to summon aid and so, as my father arrived on the scene, so too did one or two other men. It was then that more shooting began.

What happened was that while the homesteaders were discussing what had occurred, a body of men on horseback approached and stood off from them a hundred yards or more. These men then commenced firing at my father and his fellows. The homesteaders naturally returned fire and there was brisk shooting for a time, which I had heard. Then the aggressors turned tail and rode off at speed. My father had counselled against pursuit and, it being almost dawn, he had suggested that everybody return to his own home and that they would meet on the following day to see what to make of this.

'Wasn't nobody killed?' I asked with breathless excitement.

My father laughed. 'What, in the darkness and all? No.

Hitting a mark at a hundred yards is no common feat in broad daylight, never mind on a moonless night. During the war I saw two bodies of soldiers exchange fire in this way at about the same distance for above ten minutes and not one man was even wounded.'

Ma was not at all happy about all the shooting, to say nothing of where it was looking tolerably certain that there would be more of the same to come. 'I am of the opinion, Ebenezer, that we should reconsider our position.'

'If this reconsidering of position signifies that you want us to cut and run, then I am here to tell you that we will not be doing such a thing,' said Pa. 'All that is needed in this world for the villains and blackguards to take over is just what you are suggesting, running under a threat of violence. We are not leaving.'

'Do you mean then to fight with guns, like you did in the war? It is not so long since that I have forgot what it was like, not knowing from one day to the next if you had been killed. I will not go through this again for the sake of a few acres of dusty grassland.'

'It is not for the grassland. It is for more than that. I will not be driven out by a set of rascals and scamps.'

'Which is a way of saying that you are a stubborn man whose pride will force him into danger. You are not a young buck, but a family man. Will you carry on like a youngster, showing off your prowess at shooting?'

My father did not speak for a stretch, then he said, 'These are good points, Martha. I have examined my heart carefully and spoken with the Lord on this. I am stubborn, you are right, but there is more to the case here. I will not run from evildoers. We are staying.'

Ma looked searchingly at him, then went over and put her arms round him. He embraced her also and then we all had breakfast, Davy waking and crying for attention. No more was to be said on the subject.

CHAPTER 8

We now reach the part of my story where my own role in these affairs becomes more prominent. For years after the events of which I tell, I blamed myself bitterly for what happened. I have never set down the exact truth about what part I played and I still do not know how guilty I should feel. It is true that my injudicious actions perhaps provided the spark or catalyst for what ensued, but it probably would have happened anyways. If it had not concerned me it would have involved another. With two men like Anderson and my father set like flint against each other, something was bound to give. I just chanced to be the one who set the powder train alight.

I have said already that I liked to go into town on my own, partly to shirk my work, but also because it provided a break from the sheer monotony of living in the middle of nothing but grass. A week after the incident described above, the outbreak of shooting, I was granted permission to walk into Zion alone again to buy a can of lamp oil. Not much of a day out you might think, an eight mile round trip on foot, but it sure beat the hell out of

89

working in the fields. There had been no more trouble and there was cautious hope that perhaps things were going to pan out aright and that Anderson would not resort to more violence.

It was maybe two or three in the afternoon when I reached the town. I stopped first at the livery stable to exchange a little banter with the man who had sold us Dollar, our palomino.

'Good afternoon, young Maybelle,' he cried when he caught sight of me. 'And a beautiful afternoon it is too. The lark's on the wing, the snail's on the thorn, God's in his heaven and all's right with the world!'

His extravagant and flowery manner led me to suspect that he had spent lunchtime in the saloon. 'Good afternoon, Mr Carter,' I said. 'I had best not stop to talk to you. Pa says I should never speak to strange men.'

'Why, my dear Maybelle, you surely don't consider me strange?'

After a few more light-hearted words we parted company and I went to the general store. I presented my can and desired the storekeeper to sell me six gills of his oil. This done, I decided to wander round Zion a little and see what was happening.

Before I set out, my mother had impressed upon me most forcibly that I was not to go anywhere near the saloon. I guess teenage girls have not changed that much over the last hundred years or so, because no sooner had I acquired the lamp oil than I decided that the only place in town worth catching sight of was the saloon! It was a three-storey, wooden-framed building standing by itself with empty lots on both sides. I suppose that nobody much wanted premises next door to a whorehouse. Perhaps I neglected to mention that although the ground floor was a saloon, there were bedrooms up above which were rented out to various girls.

Anyways, I drifted casual like in the general direction of the saloon, being sure to stop and look at other buildings en route. This is how it is with people, especially young people, they figure that if they put on a good enough act, even though nobody's watching, it will make things OK! The saloon was not much to look at. It had been patched together from pine wood which had been painted with some dark substance such as creosote. It was not much larger than a good-sized detached house such as one might see on any street these days. In truth, it looked the most innocuous place imaginable. Well, I was young and it was broad daylight. What could possibly go wrong? Ah, the confidence of youth.

I felt a little disappointed after actually seeing the famous drinking den and cathouse at close quarters, so I decided to saunter back home by way of the livery stable and perhaps exchange a few words with the proprietor, he being practically the only person apart from Ikey and his family, whom I knew to speak to. I had been introduced to him when Pa bought Dollar and he had, I think, taken to me. I cut through one of the empty lots by the side of the saloon and as I was nearing the back of the building a small side door opened and out stumbled three drunken cowboys. I learned later that this was the entrance to the whorehouse and that some citizens felt easier about visiting the place in this discreet way, rather than passing through the saloon and walking up the staircase in full view.

'Weeell, weell,' drawled one of these rough-looking characters, 'Daddy not with you today?' He was looking at me speculatively, in a way that I did not care for, and his two companions looked as though they too might not be averse to a little fun. I tried to bluff my way out of it, frightened though I felt.

'You better not trouble me,' I said. 'My father's right across the street and I only need to call him.'

'Is that a fact?' said the cowhand. His hand shot out, grabbing me by the arm and sending the can of lamp oil flying. It splashed over his clothes. 'Ah, shit!' he exclaimed angrily. I started to pull away, too scared even to scream, I just wanted to escape.

One of the first fellow's friends said, 'Here, catch ahold of her there,' and caught my other arm in a vicious grip. It was clear that they intended to drag me out of sight round the back of the building, for what reason I could only guess at. I had never been so frightened in my life. I managed to scream once before one of the men clamped a dirty hand over my mouth. I promptly bit it. He was just raising his hand with a view to swiping me across the face, when there was an unexpected interruption.

The scuffling and my scream had attracted attention. A shadow fell across our little tableau and when I craned my head around I saw that Ikey's step-pa Al was standing a few feet away. His face gave nothing away, one could never tell much what Al was thinking. He said quietly, 'You all let that child alone now. You hear what I'm telling you?'

'Get out of here, you,' said one of the boys, 'This ain't your affair.'

'Well, you're wrong about that,' said Al, still in the same soft voice, like it might be that he was discussing the prospect of rain that afternoon. His hands shot out real sudden like and grabbed the heads of two of the cowhands. He cracked their heads together so hard that it sounded like somebody had struck an anvil. They released their grip on me and fell to the ground. The remaining boy was the only one of the three who had been carrying a weapon, a revolver in a holster at his belt. Al reached swiftly down and removed the gun. He than smashed it against the side of the man's head, before hurling the pistol to the other side of the lot.

Al put his arm round me gently, then addressed the three dazed men. 'I see or hear any of you touch this girl again,' he told them, 'and I'm going to be mighty annoyed!'

I shall leave out the aftermath of this incident, except to tell you that my mother shouted and cursed when she heard that I had been in trouble through going near the saloon. My father did not shout at all, but told me that he was shocked and surprised that I should behave in such a way. I cried on and off for the rest of the day, partly in shock at what had happened, but mainly because of how my father had spoken to me.

One result of my escapade behind the saloon was that I was forbidden to be out of sight of the house for the foreseeable future. This was no more than I expected and seemed only fair. Now, today, I can see that I came within a very whisker of getting myself raped behind that saloon and I suppose that my mother and father realized this too. Until you have children of your own, you don't know what a trouble and anxiety they can be, especially when they reach their teenage years. Here my parents were, trying to grub out a living from that bleak prairie, and contend with armed marauders, while all the time their fifteen-year-old daughter is studying only how to get into the next deadly danger! In a space of days, I had taunted and insulted a ferocious killer and put myself in the way of some degenerate types coming out of a brothel. No wonder really that Ma and Pa wanted me where they could keep an eye on what I was about.

I do not know to this very day if the incident behind the saloon made Al a target of especial hatred for Anderson and Jack Mayes. I would not be surprised. Nobody likes for their workers to be cracked round the head in that way and be unable to work for a day or two as result.

There is another point here that I have not yet drawn attention to, but which should be obvious to all those who know of that time. The Civil War had only ended ten years before the time of which I am writing. My father, Al and some of the other settlers had fought on the Union side. Anderson and Georgia Jack, though, were ardent Confederates. This created an extra area of tension in the confrontation between the two sides. I feel I should have said this earlier. It is not in reason that a diehard rebel like Jack Mayes should look kindly on any black man, let alone one who was knocking his men about.

CHAPTER 9

Two days after I had been brought home by Al, it being now Saturday, my mother expressed the wish to attend church the following morning. This did not altogether suit my father, who said, 'Is the Lord not here as well as in the church, Martha? If you would pray, cannot you do so right here and the Lord will hear you?'

'You know well enough, Ebenezer, that praising God is not a solitary activity. I wish to sing hymns and pray in the company of other God-fearing folk. I will go to the church in town.'

'There is but one church in Zion and that is not a Catholic one.'

'Nevertheless, I will still go there on Sunday. This family has not attended church for some good long while.'

I have an idea that Ma thought that a few prayers might be in order and she doubted the efficacy of appeals to the Deity that were not made in the correct place. She was not on intimate terms with the Lord as my father was, but every so often she recollected herself and

95

visited church to make up for lost time and ensure that
the maker of Heaven and Earth had not forgotten us and
our affairs.

'I have heard from Al where the pastor of this church
is, in Anderson's pocket. I am not sure that it would sit
well with me to worship in such a place.'

My mother looked at him scornfully. 'There have
always been bad priests as well as good. I dare say that the
congregation will in the main be composed of good
people. I will go to church tomorrow.'

'So be it,' said Pa.

I thought that I might be able to exploit this situation
to my advantage, saying, 'How about I look after little
Davy so that the two of you can attend church together
with no distractions? The baby's crying might otherwise
disturb you, or it might be annoy others trying to pray.'
This I thought right cunning and a way in which I could
have a morning to myself. My father though, was not
easily taken in by such stratagems. He looked at me
without speaking for a few seconds and I could tell that
he was amused by my barefaced attempts to evade divine
worship.

'This is kind of you Maybelle, but no true Christian
would object to the sound of a child in church. Did not
our Lord himself say, 'Suffer the little children to come
unto me and forbid them not'? And does it not say in
Mark's gospel, chapter ten, verse fifteen, that we must
receive the kingdom of God as little children? No, if your
mother goes to church, then we shall all go. But I am
sure your offer was well meant and I thank you for it.'

We did not take Dollar with us the next morning, but

all walked along, my mother and me taking it in turns to carry Davy. My father did not take his gun with him, saying that even unprincipled roughnecks would be unlikely to start a gunfight on the Lord's Day. I felt this to be optimistic and so, I think, did Ma, but we neither of us said anything.

Zion's one and only church was a neat, white painted wooden building, surrounded by flower beds and with a burying-ground at the back of it. It was cool and restful inside and the fittings and furnishings looked new and costly. The story my father had heard was that Anderson paid for a lot of the stuff in the church and that the minister was 'in his pocket' as the saying goes.

In fact I did not dislike the service. It was more easy-going than the ones at the Catholic church and everybody was welcome to this place. There was, though, no communion or incense or choir or any of the other things that made the Catholic worship so interesting. Anderson was there with his wife and children and he sat in a prominent place at the front in a pew of his own. I could see my father viewing this arrangement with disapproval. He was not one for anything which set some of God's people above and over others, which was, I suppose, why he preferred to pray with a few other like-minded men and not generally in a church like this.

The preacher's message was a simple one and did not endear him to Pa. His theme was that we should all be content in that station of life to which it had pleased the Lord to call us. I could see Anderson nodding his head in agreement. Have you ever noticed that the sort of men who teach this doctrine are always those whom the Lord seems to have called to a pretty comfortable station in life? You never find beggars and homeless folk declaiming about this virtue of Christian humility and acceptance of your lot in life.

After the service was over we all filed out of the church and the pastor stood at the door, saying parting words to everybody in a comfortable and self-satisfied fashion. Pa shook his hand and then asked him, 'Do you know what the prophet Amos said about protecting the widow and the orphan? He said nothing about them accepting their station in life.'

The minister looked taken aback by this and mumbled something about it needing a good deal of learning to interpret the Good Book correctly. This answer was not to my father's liking and he said, 'It is not book-learning that is required, but a humble heart, open to the Lord's instruction.'

As we moved off, Ma said to him, 'Ebenezer, why must you shame me in this way? Have you not heard that there is a time to speak and a time to remain silent?'

'Ecclesiastes three, verse five,' said my father absent-mindedly. He was looking ahead of us to where a fine carriage was waiting in the road. Standing by it were the man he knew as Jack Mayes and the red-headed young man who had accosted me in the store, the first time I visited town. Ma followed his gaze and sighed.

As we passed them the young man with red hair muttered something quietly. I could not take oath as to his very words, but they ended with 'juicy'. Young and juicy or fresh and juicy, perhaps. I felt instinctively that he was passing a personal remark about me. My father, though, heard clearly, as perhaps he was meant to. He stopped and turned towards the young man. He did not look angry, more surprised and a little disgusted, like you might be if some uncouth person broke wind next to you while you were setting at table. He walked slowly over to the red headed boy, who was grinning as if at a private joke. Ma and I watched to see how things would develop.

My pa said, 'I will not dispute with you on the Sabbath, nor yet before a house of God.'

To which the red-headed man replied, 'Yellow, eh?'

My father looked at him carefully, still not angry but as if he was examining a rare freak of nature, like the six-legged calf I once saw at a carnival sideshow. He spoke again, still in that even way. 'We may, if you so desire, discuss the colours of the rainbow. My idea, though, was that we might rather meet behind the livery stable tomorrow morning at eleven.'

The man looked doubtful, but Georgia Jack laughed and said, 'Go to it, Red. I'll second you.'

Pa turned to him and said quietly, 'Do you want to involve yourself in this affair?'

'Someone got to see there's no foul play.'

Pa nodded and said, 'So be it. We will each bring a companion to see fair play.'

Then he turned from the two ruffians and we continued walking. When once we were out of earshot, my mother said, 'So it has come to this, Ebenezer. You propose to brawl in public with a dirty cowboy. This is not a development which I hoped to see.'

'I have fought with my fists before, Martha, as we both know. It is not something I make a habit of, but you know this will not be the first time. Besides, there need be no fighting at all. If that young man offers an honest apology, then I shall shake hands with him and the matter will be closed.'

'Is that how you expect it to be?'

'To speak plainly and without chasing round the woodpile, I do not. I spoke softly to that fellow when first I met him and he was troubling our daughter here. He is one of those who takes politeness and forbearance as weakness. I must show him his error.'

I could not at this point restrain myself from adding my own contribution to the debate. 'Pa, suppose that a bunch of fellows turn up and you end up fighting not one, but twenty men.'

He smiled at me. 'Maybelle Louise, I have lived by a wood too long to be scared by the hooting of an owl.'

This did not make any kind of sense to me and seeing my bewilderment, he tried another old proverb. 'When you live with wolves, you must learn to howl.'

This was too much for my mother, who remarked, 'Quoting various old sayings will not profit you if a dozen men fall upon you tomorrow, brandishing pick-handles or, Lord forbid, one man with a rifle.'

'I have thought on this,' said my father.

The incident with the red-headed man cast somewhat of a shadow on the rest of the day.

Next morning, my father was up and at his work early. If you did not know him that well you might suppose that he had forgot the challenge he had issued to Anderson's man. I could see though that he was especially thought-ful. I guess he was figuring out how to protect himself against any sort of low dealing or double crossing which other men in Anderson's pay might be inclined to get up to. Not only that, he was also surely still considering the gunfight in which he had been involved a few nights back.

At about half past nine he set out on Dollar. I waited 'til he was out of sight, then, without asking Ma's permission, which she would not have granted, I set off on foot for Zion. I felt both afraid and excited, not knowing how events would unfold. I was also anxious that Pa would get there before me and it would all be over by the time I arrived.

I need not have worried though, because I got to town before my father and the reason, as I later learned, was this. He did not feel easy in his mind about trusting those rascally cowboys and so had called on Al and asked him to come along and keep a friendly eye on the proceedings. After all, if the man they called 'Red' was to have a second, why should my father not also have one fulfilling that office for him?

Behind the livery stable was a fenced-off enclosure like a small corral. Sometimes horses were kept here, but today it was empty. I was surprised to find a fair crowd of loafers standing around waiting for the fight to start. I guess that when you lived in a one-horse town like Zion an event of this nature was something of a crowd puller. I wondered how they had heard about it, but I don't suppose I will ever know the answer to that at this late stage. All I can tell you is that there were many men, a few women and even children standing around, to see the fun.

I mingled in with the crowd, hoping to make myself inconspicuous. I did not think my pa would take kindly to finding me here in direct disobedience of his instructions. A few minutes later the red-headed young man fetched up, accompanied by Jack Mayes and a half-dozen other cowboys. There looked to be too many onlookers from the town for them to try anything too villainous and I took it that they just come to cheer on their workmate. They joshed with 'Red', making jokes of the 'You show him!' variety. Then Pa arrived with Al.

They dismounted and Al reached out of of his saddle a beautiful, bright, new looking rifle. It was a Winchester, the 1873 model and I guess it must have cost Al a fortune. He did not wave it around, but walked with my father over to the group of Anderson's men with it tucked casually under his arm. There were a few words exchanged which I did not hear. My father later told Ma that he had requested the young man to apologize for his insulting words about me and that Red had declined to do so. Al and my father then walked a short distance to the other side of the corral and prepared for the contest.

Pa unbuckled his belt and left it with his pistol in Al's keeping. He then took off his shirt as well and advanced into the enclosure, which now took on the aspect of some Roman arena, where a bloody combat was to take place. Red also discarded his shirt and walked up to my father. There had been a low hum of conversation, but this died away as the two men squared off. Red was taller than my father, but whereas Pa had a quiet and reserved dignity about him, Red had the air of a man who was reckless and arrogant. He turned to his friends and smiled. Then he swung his fist at my father's face. Pa knocked the arm aside gracefully and then delivered a mighty blow to the young man's jaw. Red staggered backwards and my father followed up this first blow with another, which connected with the red-headed man's eye. He keeled over, unconscious, and the fight looked to be over.

My father turned away from the scene and began walking back towards the corner where Al was waiting. Jack Mayes had in the meantime scrambled through the wooden railings and come up behind my father.

'Cade!' he called to him. Pa stopped and turned to face him.

'I have no desire to fight you. That fellow was exceedingly discourteous to my daughter and I felt need to reprove him. The matter is ended and I have ploughing to do.'

'Discourteous, hey?' said Mayes, 'Well I say you're a lying, yellow-bellied coward, your wife's a pox-ridden whore and your daughter looks to be following the same road as her ma, consorting with black men and such. That discourteous enough for you?'

This was all said loudly, so that all those hanging on the fence could hear every word. There was little my father could do after this except take the challenge. He said to Mayes, 'Will you take off your shirt and set to with me?'

'You're damn right,' said Georgia Jack, removing his shirt and tossing it aside. Then he and my father went at it.

Now I dare say that you have from time to time seen men throwing punches at each other in a bar-room brawl. They trade a few blows, maybe kick each other and then the thing subsides. This was not at all what happened between Jack Mayes and my father. Pa may have had an advantage in height, but what he lacked in size, Mayes made up for in wiriness and grit. It was a fearful thing to see two strong men striking at each other's faces in a protracted bout of violence. You could hear the sound as their fists struck home and after a few minutes blood began to flow from my father's nose where one of Jack Maye's blows had caught him.

I would say that the two men were fighting fairly for around ten or fifteen minutes. There was of course no timekeeper, so they did not break every few minutes. The end of the fight came when, as I have so often observed to be the case, a wicked person's actions recoiled upon him.

Jack Mayes had fought pretty fairly, as had my father. There was in those days for fights of this nature an unspoken agreement that the fighting would be limited to blows with the clenched fist and that there would be no kicking, head-butting, strangling, eye-gouging or any other such tricks. I do not know what prompted him to attempt such a thing, but after one flurry of punches had taken place and they had backed off from each other, Georgia Jack tried to kick my father between the legs. The consequence was not as he had expected, because Pa not only knocked his leg aside, he also grabbed hold of Mayes's ankle and twisted his leg sharply to one side, causing Jack Mayes to fall to the ground and lie for a moment on his back. In an instant, my father was standing over him, with his boot pressed down on the fallen man's throat. He stood like this for a few seconds, looking down gravely at his vanquished adversary.

'How are you doing down there?' enquired my father solicitously. 'You getting enough air?'

In truth, it did not look at all as though Jack Mayes was getting anywhere near enough air, because he was beginning to go purple in the face under the pressure of my father's foot. He clasped at the ankle, but Pa was putting much of his weight on Mayes's neck, so the attempt was ineffectual.

'I will tell you a thing,' said my father. 'I don't look for you to cross my path again, Mayes. For me, this affair finishes right now. Did you say something?' This was, I assume, meant in a jocular way, as the man could not breathe, let alone speak. 'I hope we are clear now,' said my father, lifting his foot and walking back towards where Al stood.

Then things happened very fast. As Pa walked away, Jack Mayes choked and coughed, then his hand dived down towards his boot. At the same moment Al vaulted over the fence, ran to Mayes and, reversing his Winchester, drove the butt hard into the side of Mayes's head, so clubbing the man insensible. As he did this, a couple of the more hot-blooded cowboys jumped over the fence into the corral. Al's response was to hold on to the cocking lever of the rifle and then kind of flip the Winchester in the air while keeping a hold of the lever. This had the effect of cocking his piece and he then, with one smooth motion, brought the butt to his hip so that he was covering the cowboys. He shook his head warningly at them. Then, while everybody was watching, he reached down and lifted something from Mayes's hand. It was a little derringer pistol. The murderous rogue obviously carried it in his boot and had drawn it with the intention of shooting my father in the back.

Al held the pistol aloft so that everybody in the crowd could see it and understand both why he had acted as he did and also what sort of man Jack Mayes was. Then he dropped the derringer and went over to my father, arriving just as I did.

'Maybelle Louise, you will be the death of me,' was my father's greeting to me. 'Did you not hear my express instruction that you were to remain at home? What am I to do with you?' Then he turned to Al. 'You saved my life this day. My family seems to cause you little but trouble and draw you into danger, but I am right grateful to you. You have been a true friend.'

Al treated what had happened lightly, saying, 'You would do the same in my place, Ebenezer.' He turned to me, saying, 'Maybelle, you are always at the eye of the storm; how is that?'

I did not reply. On the way home I expected Pa to be angry with me, but oddly he was not. In fact he ruffled my hair and said that I was a torment to him and he wished he had had a boy instead. I think the way of it was this: although not a boastful man or given to showing off, he had not been displeased for his daughter to witness how he had bested two ruffians, one after the other.

My ma was more forthright in her denunciation of my conduct, telling my father that this was a direct consequence of his never having whipped me as a child. However, she too was keen to hear the details of the fight and I could see that she was as proud of Pa as I was myself.

CHAPTER 10

When the real trouble started it was a lot more brutal and direct than my father expected. I believe that he thought that Anderson would try and provoke a dispute with one of the homesteaders when they were in town, away from their land. For what he really planned, though, the town might have furnished too many witnesses and he was still making himself out as the law, a man devoted to keeping the peace.

After Al had gone home and my father had thanked him warmly once more for his help, we sat up 'til late talking and being sociable. I seemed to have escaped censure for going to watch my father's fight and everything was appearing fine. It was pitch dark and about eleven of the clock, when we heard two shots in quick succession.

'That came from the direction of Al's house or I miss my guess,' said Pa. He reached down the shotgun and handed me his pistol. 'Martha, fetch the baby. Maybelle, you and your mother and brother go down to the river. Keep your back to it and then you will see anybody

108

coming towards you. I don't want you trapped in here where anybody knows you might be. There is some mischief afoot.'

With that my father was gone and we walked down to the riverbank and waited. After an hour or so, which my mother and I spent chatting in a desultory fashion of the disadvantages of being caught up in a range war, he returned. 'It is all right,' he told us. 'Nobody has been hurt.'

It turned out that Al had heard someone prowling round the back of his place and when he went out to investigate somebody discharged a firearm in his direction. Al, though, had taken the precaution of carrying out his Winchester with him and he returned fire, as far as he knew only with the effect of driving away any intruders and without actually hitting anybody. We went soberly to bed that night, conscious that the danger to us and our neighbours had not yet subsided. This was brought home forcefully to us the next morning, while we were having breakfast.

First we heard about it was when Al rode over with another man whom I did not know, but who had met my father before. Al introduced him as Caleb Watson, who lived a couple of miles from us. It was a beautiful morning and we were sitting outside eating our porridge when they rode up. 'Will you have a bite to eat?' enquired my father, gesturing towards the pot, although truth to tell it contained barely enough for the four of us, never mind anybody else. Al dismounted and walked over to where we were sitting.

'Tom Dillon was killed last night,' he announced

sombrely. 'Somebody just knock on his door after dark and shoot him down when he open the door. After I drove them off, they must have gone searching for a softer target.'

Pa cast a look at me and my mother. 'Let's step over here's a pace, Al—' he began to say.

'You set right where you are, Ebenezer Cade,' Ma told him, 'There's been enough whispering and secret conversations taking place since we moved out of Pittsburgh. Let Al tell us all what's what.'

Caleb Watson, who had not got off his horse, spoke. 'His wife didn't see who shot him. She said there was two or three of them and they all had cloths tied round they mouths. Nobody speak to Tom, just shoot him as soon as he open the door.' Al and my father looked round at him irritably. Al seemed about to speak, but my mother cut in again.

'What are you all planning to do?'

'First off,' said Pa, 'is where we will not be doing anything whatsoever in a hurry. We need to have facts.'

'Facts?' said Caleb Watson. 'Is what the hell more facts you needing, Ebenezer? Fact is, the man dead.'

'It may be so,' said my father, in the same calm way that he would talk about a mouse getting at a sack of grain. 'Is anything known about Tom Dillon's life before he come here? Could this be some business that follow him here and have nothing at all to do with the case of Anderson?'

It was plain as a pikestaff that this had not occurred to anybody else. Al and Caleb looked at each other and shook their heads slowly. 'It's the hell of a coincidence,' opined Caleb Watson soberly. 'Just when we expecting trouble, along comes a band of gunmen and they then assassinate our neighbour. You think that a coincidence, Ebenezer? Especially where this happen just after Al here knock out Anderson's foreman and then is himself shot at in the middle of the night. That is some coincidence.'

'I don't think anything on the matter at all yet,' said my father quietly. 'What is happening to his wife?' Nobody knew.

After a little more discussion it was decided that my father would saddle up Dollar and ride over with Caleb and Al to Tom Dillon's home and see what the situation amounted to. I have said before that my father was not a man to be hasty or intemperate and, even after a cold blooded murder of this sort, he was not about to be stampeded into taking any action without thinking through on it carefully beforehand. He intended to establish all the facts of the case first. After he had ridden off my mother said, 'Maybelle, what is your opinion about staying here? I mean, when looked at side by side with returning to Pittsburgh?' I did not know what to reply to this.

'I don't know, Ma. Why are you asking?'

'My family were not over keen on my marrying Ebenezer. You have most likely heard this before?'

I shrugged, a bit embarrassed like. I did not really know what my mother wanted me to say and I didn't like hearing things about my parents from before I was born.

'Ebenezer could have a job in my father's company, Maybelle, any time that he cared to take it. My own mother and father always wanted us, when once we were married, to move to Boston to be near them. Ebenezer, your pa, he always said no, it was for a man to keep his own family and not depend upon anybody else. He is a proud man.' She said this last as though pride were not always a good thing.

'We will not talk of this matter further for now,' Ma said. 'Just set in your mind what I say, that we might do worse than return to the East and possibly even go to Boston. Folk there are not prone to being shot down when they answer their door of an evening, not by a long sight.'

'All right, Ma, I'll remember.' I hugged her, something which I seldom did.

To cut a long story short, it seems that Tom Dillon, the dead man, had led an exemplary and blameless life in New York before deciding to try his luck in Nebraska. He had only been settled here less than a twelvemonth before he was killed. It was pretty sure that Anderson had caused his death, a supposition which became nigh on a certainty the following week, when he gave the dead man's widow fifty dollars so that she could return to New York. Soon as she had left, right after the funeral, we learned that Anderson was putting it around in Zion that one of his men had staked legal claim to the 160 acres which had belonged to Tom Dillon. For the fifty dollars, the dead man's wife had signed what she might have taken for a receipt, but was in fact a legal document relinquishing her claim to the land. This came to light later. The soddy itself had been torn down and all the little bits of fence pulled up. Clearly, Anderson hoped to return all the small farms to being open range.

So this was now the state of play in the area surrounding the town of Zion. Two homesteaders had been killed, one by some sort of trial and the other by plain banditry. By the by, there was a slight mystery as to why nobody had heard the shots that killed Tom Dillon. An examination of his dead body showed that he had been killed with a very small-calibre weapon, perhaps just a .22 pistol, what some would call a ladies' gun. This would have made a pop little louder than a firecracker. Thoughts turned to that derringer of Jack Mayes. Anderson had got his man to stake claim on the dead man's land and had then freed it up and returned it to open range. It was fairly obvious that he hoped so to frighten the rest of us into running off, which would give him the opportunity to stake claim to our land as well.

Although I was no more than a child at that time, it occurred to me to wonder why Anderson had not just staked claim to these parts before we all came along and settled up the valley. Why wait until we were already living here before going through all this rigmarole and murder? I asked my father on it after the killing of Tom Dillon.

'The case lies in this wise,' my father told me. 'The people who allocated us this land are the Federal Government in Washington. They have, I suppose, a big map there and can point to this or that territory and declare it as being open and free to settle. This is, as you might say, the big picture. Howsoever, if some unfortunate farmer happen to drop dead while ploughing his field, Washington do not wish to receive word of this misfortune. They look to the local authorities to deal with the event and allow another person to lay claim to the dead man's property. Anderson is what you might call a big man in these parts, but a person of small account in Washington, were he to go there. He therefore waits for the land to be settled and then relies upon his cunning and corrupt ways to win him the field. In short, I have no doubt that he bribes somebody in the state capital to allocate a claim to one of his henchmen. In this wise, he is confident of winning against us in the end.'

'But Pa, ain't there nothing to stop such a man? Seems to me Anderson and people like him can do as they pleases.'

'That is how the world sees the case, Maybelle,' my father replied, stroking his beard thoughtfully. 'But there is two things for you to think on. Firstly, is where God does not take kindly to such goings on, as you would know if you spent a little more of your spare time reading scripture and a little less getting into various scrapes and going flat against my instructions to you. The other point, Maybelle, touches upon what I have already told you when Anderson and that blackguard foreman of his favoured us with a visit, soon after we arrived in these here parts. Namely, that if there is any shoving and disputing, then the man with a calm and steady nerve who is carrying a firearm, that man will generally come out against others who are not so well equipped.'

In practical terms, all this meant that my father and neighbours doubled up their patrols from two men to three or four at a time and that nobody went alone into Zion during the day or at all after dark. This hardly affected me, because my father had given it as his ruling that I was not to go into town at all except in his company and under his direct personal supervision. I guess these days it would not be easy for the father of a teenaged girl to insist upon such conditions, but in them days it seemed quite natural. I could see that after all that had happened, it would in any case be foolhardy for me to hazard myself alone in that town again.

You might be wondering why folk in the town were not getting a little edgy at all this business, the shooting dead of a farmer and so on. The answer to that shows what a cunning man Anderson was. He put the story about that we homesteaders were a regular set of libertines and that Tom Dillon had been killed in a quarrel over a woman.

Forty eight hours after Tom Dillon was shot his funeral was held. The church in Zion had a small burying-ground, but people often preferred to inter the departed closer to their home. So it was that we and about thirty other people gathered on the edge of Tom Dillon's land to bury him there. By common consent, my father had been chosen to conduct the service. There had been some talk of engaging the minister from Zion to do the job, but he was not popular with most of us farmers.

It was a bright, sharp June morning when we buried Tom Dillon. There was no question of a coffin; the deceased was wrapped in a length of stout canvas. I shouldn't think the grave was the traditional six foot deep either. Still, there we stood, gathered politely round the hole, with the corpse laid on the ground by the side. My father had his Bible with him and he read the relevant parts of the burial service. 'Man that is born of woman . . . he cometh forth like a flower . . . in my

father's house there are many mansions . . . I am the res-
urrection and the life. . . .' And so on and so forth.

In addition to conducting the service my father had
been asked to say a few words. Something I have noticed
about funerals these days is that they are usually fairly
tame and civilized affairs. The minister stands up and
says his piece, then some relative might say a few words
about what a kind and loving person the dead person
was. Then it's back to somebody's house for ham sand-
wiches and sherry. Well, let me tell you, things were not
always done in such a polite way. I have not, for example,
for many years seen any grieving individual jump into the
grave and lie on the coffin moaning. Nor have I noticed
any deadly blood feuds begin as a result of 'a few words'
at the graveside.

The repercussions of the 'few words' spoken at a
funeral could last for years when I was a girl. Everyone is
keyed up and then somebody delivers what somebody
else takes as a slight upon the dear departed. 'Fore you
know it, somebody threatening one of the mourners with
retribution of a sanguinary kind and a few days later
there is shooting, or at the very least a fistfight. Like I say,
things seem now to be a deal calmer than was once the
case, with even the nearest and dearest comporting
themselves with dignity.

Anyways, be that as it may, Tom Dillon's widow was one
of those who tried to throw herself into the grave. She
was restrained from this rash action by assorted females
who laid hands upon her, speaking comfortable words
quietly as my father cleared his throat and prepared to
deliver what they call a eulogy. This he did not have the

chance to do. While Tom Dillon's widow was being soothed and embraced by various people and as my father waited for everybody to settle down, there was an unexpected interruption. This took the form of somebody loosing off a couple of shots from the rise of land a couple of hundred yards away.

I cannot think that the intention was really to shoot anybody. After all, when you draw down on a party of perhaps thirty souls at that range, then your chances of hitting somebody are good, even if you are just aiming in their general direction. In fact the bullets kicked up the earth about thirty feet away from us. There was a mad scramble to fall to the ground or take cover behind the wagon used to bring the body to the burying place. Now being a funeral and all, the men had thought it more respectful to refrain from carrying weapons. It had not occurred to anybody that someone might be so lost to common decency as to disrupt a funeral in this fashion. But there it was. My father had identified the direction from which the shots had come and had cast me and my ma to the ground. He made us lie down so that he could interpose his own body between us and the source of gunfire. I was holding Davy in my arms and he wasn't none to keen on the proceedings any more than the rest of us.

After a space, it became apparent that there was not going to be any more shooting. Everybody then commenced to get up and dust theyselves down. There was a certain amount of strong language from some of the men.

'Those murdering sons of bitches!' exclaimed Caleb

Watson. I had seen him duck behind the wagon mighty fast when the shooting started, leaving his wife standing out in the open. Perhaps he was afraid that others had seen this evidence of his cowardliness and he proposed to make up for it by bluster and strong language.

'Caleb,' said my father mildly, 'do not forget that there are women and children present here.'

Watson looked at him balefully. 'It's all well and good you talking like some kind of preacher now, Ebenezer. It was you as got everything stirred up here, which is why Tom here got killed.'

This is so often the way with weak and cowardly men, as I have noticed time and again over the years. They lash out and try and blame anyone rather than their own selves for what is happening. You will recollect that when he brought news of Tom Dillon's murder, this same man was fired up and accusing my father of shilly shallying. Now he was suggesting that my father had been too hasty and thus precipitated the current problems with Anderson. Pa said nothing, but issued a few brief instructions to those around him.

'You men had best take your families home now,' he said. 'Maybe you could all then meet me down by the river on the edge of my fields. We will then talk this over and decide what is to be done. Matters cannot continue like this.' He spoke quietly and reassuringly as if they were to meet and plan a church fête or some such. His next words dispelled this impression though. 'You had all best make sure you do not come unarmed.'

When we got home my father took down his gunbelt and buckled it on. Ma watched him and then said,

'Ebenezer, I have been considering matters and this is what I have thought. We could do a sight worse than go back East and make a start somewhere else. Maybe Boston.'

'Boston is not part of this question,' announced my father, quietly but definitely. 'I do not propose to consider anything which tends in that direction.'

'It is a nice city. You know it is, Ebenezer. We could live in a fine apartment, not in a hut such as this, which a Red Indian would be ashamed to call his home.'

'Red Indians are neither here nor there,' said Pa. 'We are not going to Boston and I wonder that you feel it time to raise this issue again. We have talked before of this and my opinion has not changed.'

'You mean that I have talked of it and you have remained silent,' observed my mother sharply. 'Your stubbornness is well and good in some causes, but I am afeared that this time it will result in more deaths. I say we should go to Boston.'

'We will talk on this later,' my father said. 'I must now go and meet our neighbours. We must think on what is to be done.'

Which left me and my mother and baby Davy alone in the soddy. I will say this for my mother, looking at the thing with the hindsight of one who has herself had daughters and experienced all the grief that a wilful adolescent can occasion she was trying hard to get close to me. I do not think that it was just that she wanted to win me over to her point of view on the Boston scheme; I think that she really wanted us to be closer than we had been in recent months and years.

'Maybelle, I have a bad feeling for this affair. I believe that if things continue in this wise, more people are apt to get killed. I am afeared that one of them will be your pa.'

There was not much that I could say to this. I went over to Ma and put my arm round her shoulders, comforting her like. 'It will be all right, Ma,' I told her. 'Pa knows what is what and he will find a way through this.'

'Is this hut and those stony fields worth the fight though? That is the sort of question we should be answering here, not if'n your pa is a better hand with firearms than a set of drunken cowhands.'

This was such a neat summing up of the entire situation that I could not think of anything more to say on the subject. Although my mother could be quite childlike at times, this very character of hers sometimes gave her the ability to sum things up in a way that a more mature and intelligent person could not do. There was no more to be said on this particular topic and so we busied ourselves with getting the midday meal ready.

When Pa returned he seemed very thoughtful and not inclined to talk overmuch until we had all eaten, which we did sitting on the ground outside. After we had finished he lit his pipe and sat staring moodily at nothing in particular. We could see that he was thinking hard. At last he said to me, 'Maybelle, do you wish to visit town tomorrow?'

'Yes please, Pa. Are we going to the blacksmiths?'

'No, we are going to the church.' He saw my face fall. I was not a great one for church at that stage in my life, although I have remedied that in recent years and done enough praying to make up for a largely godless youth.

'I will tell you about this, Maybelle. And you too, Martha.' He added this last hastily, as he saw the look on my mother's face. 'While I was talking to our neighbours, one of Anderson's men rode up. He was polite and respectful and asked that I would go to town and speak to his boss tomorrow morn. We are to meet in the church and talk matters over. I think that Anderson suggested the church to reassure me. Even those scoundrels would, I think, stop short of gunplay in or around a sacred edifice. It will be safe.'

'This is well enough,' said my mother, 'but where does Maybelle fit into this scheme. Did he ask to be introduced to her?'

My father did not speak for few seconds. Then he said, 'No. That is my own idea. It is my experience that when a child is present during a meeting, it tends towards making the overall tone softer and more restrained. I do not want high words spoken at this talk and I feel that having a young girl around would make even Anderson moderate hisself. It will go towards making it a more civilized business if Anderson is introduced to my child. This is at least how I see the case.'

'I don't like it, Ebenezer,' said Ma.' I do not trust this man. Such a one who would break up a funeral with gunfire will not scruple to shoot a man in church. I do not like this at all.'

'I wish to find a peaceful way from this. I must make at least an effort to that end. Me and Maybelle will go to Zion tomorrow.'

121

CHAPTER 11

After breakfast the next day my father and I set off towards Zion. My mother was quiet during the time we were eating and then, as we were about to leave, she took Pa to one side. 'I will tell you now, Ebenezer,' she said, 'that I do not like this. There is something amiss about the whole thing which sits ill with me. Still and all, I know you for a man who will have his own way. Promise me that you will not let anything befall our daughter.'

'Whatever is between me and Anderson will not affect Maybelle. She will be as safe as if she were here with you. Trust me now, Martha.'

'If you cannot come to an arrangement with this man, will you then consider on what I have said to you concerning Boston?'

'We will talk of all this later, Martha. For now me and Maybelle must be on our way.'

It was a beautiful morning and truly a pleasure to be travelling on such a day. We took Dollar with us and my father was content for me to ride him while he himself walked alongside. I chattered in the light and inconsequential way that girls of that age are prone to do. I asked him why he was not wearing his gun.

'If the plan is to murder me, Maybelle,' he said, 'then that end could be achieved by a man with a rifle up on yonder ridge.' I looked nervously in the direction he indicated. He laughed. 'Nobody is going to shoot anybody today. Your mother is right to be wary of this man. He and his foreman are natural born killers. But they will not act today. Anderson wishes to see if we will leave peaceably, perhaps with the passage of money to ease the way. It is only when he is sure that this will not happen that he will resort again to plain murder. I do not look for trouble today, so just enjoy the ride.'

It took us maybe an hour and a half to reach town. There was no road; the journey meant weaving through the fields and land of people living between us and Zion. A couple of times my father stopped to exchange greetings with men working their land. The men we spoke to were both wearing pistols. One of them raised his eyebrows questioningly and asked what was what when he noticed that my father was unarmed. Pa said the same as he had said to me and my mother.

The white-painted church looked as pretty as a picture. At that time, the wooden buildings were generally coated with creosote to preserve them, rather than painted. The effect was that all the other buildings in town were a dark brown and the church shone out pure white. Even the picket fence around the burying ground had been painted white and there were flowers planted outside. It looked a bright and inviting place.

I believe that I have already said that Zion became a 'ghost town' in later years, because it was not close enough to the railroad. Well, sometime in the twenties, about fifty years after these events, I visited Nebraska and my son took me in search of the old town. It was all but vanished. Most every building had collapsed and rotted away. The only exception was the church. It looked pretty weather-beaten and dilapidated, but it was still standing. We went inside, but the feelings and memories were so powerful, even after the passage of such a length of time, that I had to leave almost at once. I have not been back since that day in 1924.

We left Dollar at the livery stable, I forget now what it was, but some trifling matter needed to be attended to with him. We then walked to the church and went inside to wait for Anderson. I could not help but observe that for all his reassuring words to everybody, my father was keeping a sharp eye out all around him, watching people closely as if to see whether he could detect any hostile intent in them. Everything seemed quiet and peaceful though. Inside, the church smelled of polish. No expense had been spared in furnishing the interior and I would think that few of those worshipping there had any such beautiful furniture at home as the pews, table and pulpit to be found there. I do not recollect what precise denomination this church was, but it was not Catholic, that I do know. It looked a little too comfort-able and well kept for any of the stricter and more puritanical sects that were common at that time.

We did not have long to relax and admire the inside of the building. Long enough for my father to remove his hat, though, and fall to his knees before the table which served as an altar. I sat down behind him and tried to look as though I too had my mind fixed upon more spiritual matters! It was in this way that Anderson found us when he entered the church a few minutes after we had ourselves arrived. He was so prompt that I guessed, and my father later told me that he also had thought this, that Anderson must have been in the town already and watching the church for our arrival. He seemed embarrassed to discover my father kneeling like he was, talking to the Lord in a low, businesslike voice as though he were trying to strike an agreement with some particularly hard bargainer.

Anderson had taken off his own hat when he entered the church and nodded amiably to me. When my father showed no signs of having noticed his presence, although I will take oath that he had spotted Anderson at once, the great landowner cleared his throat like he had come into a hardware store and the assistants were all out the back and nobody minding the counter.

Pa spoke a last few words to the Deity, closing whatever deal he had put before the maker of Heaven and Earth, before standing up and turning to face Anderson. That man smiled fulsomely and approached my father, putting out his hand. They shook and then my father introduced me. Anderson was full of oil and guile and I remember thinking that this was not a man whom I would trust an inch. Let somebody fall dead in the street and, if no one was around, Anderson would be the sort of fellow who would prise open the corpse's mouth to see if there was any gold in there worth stealing. He was a plain blackguard and that is all that I shall say of him.

This all took place almost a century ago, but I still feel

the same hatred and contempt for that man. There have been many people over the years whom I have fell out with, but after a few years I hardly remember what those arguments were about. If I met any of those folk now, like as not I would smile and greet them cheerfully. Not Anderson, though. I tell you now before God, if I met that man I would serve him again as I did in 1875. Of which, more later.

'It strikes me, Mr Cade,' said Anderson, after he and my father had settled down next to each other in a pew, 'Strikes me as though you and me got off on the wrong foot when first we met. I regret that, I truly do. I am hoping that we might now come to some sort of amicable arrangement.'

'That is well spoken,' said my father cautiously. 'Perhaps there has been some hasty action taken. I am not a man who goes hunting for trouble and if you can show me a way from this difficulty of ours, I shall be glad to take it.'

'I have been thinking this through carefully.' said Anderson, giving my father a sidelong glance, which seemed to me to have a deal of cunning about it. 'I have come up with an idea and I should like to see what you say on it.'

'I am always ready to hear a reasonable man speak.'

'You surely know, Cade – Mr Cade, I mean – how I am placed. I cannot get my herds to the water, I cannot even let them roam the range any more because of all the little fences and fields which you and your neighbours have erected. Would you not say that this is true?'

My father said nothing, but watched Anderson closely

to see what would follow.

'What I propose is,' said Anderson, 'that we, which is to say you and me, come to some agreement now on this. I am not an unreasonable man, nor am I a poor one. Many of those men in that valley where you have your land are barely grubbing out a living. Let me tell you frankly, if we get a hard winter, some of they families will starve.'

'I have misjudged you,' said my father in an expressionless voice. 'I did not have you pegged for a philanthropist. Are you aiming to help those struggling men out?'

'You have hit upon it exactly,' said Anderson, smiling. 'That is just what I wish to do. Listen, here is what I suggest. I shall put forward a sum of money, which you can distribute as you see fit, in order to help some of those sad cases to leave this area and return to where they came from. I am sure that most of them will be happier so.

'You can continue living where you are, I will even supply you with lumber to build yourselves a proper home to live in, rather than the pig-pens which you are currently inhabiting. But you will then work for me, drawing a right good wage without all the uncertainty of farming as you are now, not knowing where the next meal is likely to come from. What do you say?' He looked at my father eagerly, almost greedily.

'What you are suggesting,' said my father slowly, 'amounts to this. You wish to clear the valley of all the homesteaders, along with their homes, families, fences and fields. In return, you say that I can remain, but will be employed by you on the same basis as your cowhands and so on. Have I understood you correctly?'

Anderson was smiling and nodding his head rapidly the while. 'Yes, yes, that is exactly so, Cade. I see we understand each other very well.'

'You are by some accounts that I have heard, a man who attends church regular on Sunday. I have at any rate seen you there myself on one occasion.'

Anderson looked puzzled and a little taken aback. 'Yes, that is so. But I do not see how that connects with the current business.'

'It is connected in this wise,' said my father calmly. 'You have a hankering for some land which does not belong to you. In order to possess yourself of that land, you will kill, cheat and lie. You will bribe men. Now you think that you have hit upon an easier scheme. You think that by killing one or two men as a warning, you can now engage me in your plans to help do your work for you. And my return on the affair will be to become your bondsman.' He stood up and looked down at Anderson, peering into his face intently, as though it were a difficult book that he was trying to puzzle out. 'You put me in mind of King Ahab and how as he took a liking to Naboth's vineyard. You are a bad man, Anderson, and I would sooner treat with a rattlesnake than have dealings with you.' He turned to me. 'Come, Maybelle.'

Anderson's syrupy tone changed in an instant. 'Why, you stubborn jackass!' he said in a strangled voice, like he had crammed too much in his mouth and was on the point of choking. 'I tried to deal square with you, Cade. And all you give me in return is brag and bluster. So be it. Remember that you had a right good deal offered to you and threw it back in my face. Just you remember that!'

Pa looked at him calmly. 'I am not apt to forget this.'

We left the church and went back to the livery stable. Standing outside the church were two of Anderson's men. One of them smiled at me as we passed and I ignored him. My father saw the man's smile and turned to stare at him. The smile faded from the man's face and he looked searchingly at my father to see if there was going to be trouble. I think now that Anderson had brought these men as bodyguards, just in case my father had been planning any dirty tricks. That's how it is with treacherous and untrustworthy men; they are always expecting others to behave in the same low way as them themselves. They judge other men by their own standards. As the Bible tells us, *The wicked flee when none pursueth*. I was worried about what I had heard in the church.

'Pa, what will he do now?'

'I do not know, Maybelle, and that's the God's honest truth. Something in the murdering and stealing line, I should not be surprised. He hoped to settle the matter with money, but now he will use violence, or I miss my guess.'

'Are we going to go to Boston, Pa?'

My father stopped dead and turned to face me. 'We are not going to Boston under any circumstances or conditions. Boston is not now, nor has it ever been part of the equation in my plans for the future.'

'So we are stopping right here?'

'Yes, we are stopping right here!'

When we returned home Ma could see right away from the sober look of my father that things had not gone as well as they might. She did not ask a lot of questions, but gave us some food. After the meal she said, 'I can see Ebenezer, without your telling me, that this has not turned out as you might have wished. What are we now to expect of that murderous scoundrel? Will there be more bloodshed?'

'I am not looking to shed any man's blood. If another man seeks to shed mine, then so be it. I am setting right here on my land. I will not trouble anybody, and if anybody troubles me, well then it may be a bad business.'

'Ebenezer, I will ask you again. Can I not at least take the children to Boston until we see how it is going to be here?'

'We are a family, Martha. I have seen cases where families split up and it is no good for anybody. It always turns out to be a bad business. We will stay here.'

Ma could see that there was nothing more to be said about it. My father would not shout and rave, but neither would he back down if he felt he was right. He was like a hill or tree. Just set in place and impossible to move. He did not need to raise his voice because he knew that he would not move from the position which he had adopted. There are very few men like that in the world, men who simply know they are right and do not care to debate the question. Some might call it, as Anderson had done, stubbornness.

On the evening of the day that me and my Pa had met Anderson in the church a few men called by our house.

These men had somehow heard what had chanced when we met Anderson and wanted to know how it might alter things now. My father told them that it might be no bad idea if the patrols were increased, so that six men instead of three or four were prowling about at any one time. Any shooting would be the signal for all able-bodied men to converge on the scene of such and stand to, ready to assist. It was I think, plain to all involved that this could not be kept up for very long. All the men were working hard from dawn to dusk, tending their land. They needed a good long rest at night, not to be riding out on the scout like this half the night.

For the next few days, maybe three or four, I don't recall precisely, this is how it went: everybody working like fury during the day and then riding the range at night. My father tried to arrange it so that men only had to go on patrol one night in three, but this was not always possible and there was a lot of grumbling and complaints of unfairness. This again is how things often are in this world. A man who takes the trouble to organize and take care of his fellows is all too often criticized and abused as a slave-driver and tyrant. My father would not accept weak excuses from men anxious to evade their turn at guard duty and did more than anybody else.

CHAPTER 12

On maybe the third or fourth night after we met Anderson, try as he might, my father could only get two men to agree to patrol the area. He himself had been out two nights running to make up the shortfalls of men not over-eager to do their share. He could not spend a third consecutive night in the saddle, but blamed himself bitterly. We went to sleep that night, unaware of what was developing. Next morning when I woke up, I went out back to answer a call of nature. As soon as I left the house I could smell burning, like someone had had a big bonfire. I went back inside and woke my pa. I told him that I could smell burning and he was up and out in a few seconds. He had been sleeping in his clothes, perhaps expecting his sleep to be disturbed.

We went outside and both sniffed the early morning air, trying to gauge where the smell might be coming from. There was a light easterly breeze and the two homes in that direction were Al's and another man's whose name I do not recollect and who does not feature in this account. Pa went and saddled up Dollar and told me to stay and help my mother. Then he set off at a canter towards Al's place. I followed, half-running and half-walking briskly. As I approached the top of the rise, I could see at once where the smell was coming from. In the distance, I could see a thin haze drifting up from the soddy where Al lived with Ikey. Even at a mile or so, I could see that something was terribly wrong. It was only as I drew closer that the full horror of the thing was evident to me.

My father had dismounted and was surveying the scene grimly when I arrived. He had seen enough to want to spare me, because he waved me back and told me to go home. For once, I ignored him completely. This is what I saw. The farm wagon, table and chairs from inside the house and probably everything else that would burn, had been piled up and set alight. Half the front of the soddy had been pulled down to make it uninhabitable. Al's horse and oxen were lying dead in front of the house, in such large pools of blood as to suggest that they had had their throats cut. Near by were Al and his wife, also dead. It looked to me like they had been stabbed. Worst of all was where the roof and front of the soddy had been pulled down to expose the central beam, the roof ridge, which ran about twelve foot off the ground and supported the roof. From this was hanging Ikey. The whole, entire family had been killed.

Seeing the dead livestock and Al was bad, but seeing Ikey hanging there was too much for me. I stumbled off and threw up. My father came after me and held back my hair out of the way as I retched and vomited. I could not have imagined anything such, even in my worst dreams.

After a spell, I had finished and I walked off and sat down with my back to the hideous scene.

'Why would they do such a thing, Pa?'

'Because if this does not drive away a few more of the families here, then I miss my guess,' replied my father. 'This is the best thing that Anderson could have done, given the circumstances that he is in. Also considering what happened in town recently, he had a score to settle here anyways.'

This had not occurred to me. 'You mean, this might be my fault?'

My father shook his head. 'It was not your fault, Maybelle. Anderson had it in mind to kill somebody if I would not go along with him. This is the result. If he had not killed Al and his family, it would have been Caleb, perhaps. This is to be laid at Anderson's account, not yours.'

At the time I was mighty relieved to hear this and for some years believed it to be true. At a later stage in my life though, I came to think that my thoughtless action in wandering behind that saloon caused the death of Al and his family as sure as if I had took a gun and shot them. I know that Al also struck Jack Mayes with the butt end of a rifle, but those other three cowboys that Al knocked about would also have had a powerful grudge against him. Even ninety-odd years later, it is not clear to me to what extent I was to answer for those deaths.

My father cut down Ikey and laid him out next to his ma and step-pa. Then he looked round a bit, searching for clues that would enable anybody to lay this squarely at the door of Anderson and his men. There was nothing

134

to indicate who might have been behind it. As my father later figured it, there must have been at least three hands involved here. Al must have been taken by surprise, because he had been stabbed repeatedly in the back. His wife had been slashed in the throat and Ikey knocked about a bit before they strung him up. Most likely, Al had been jumped as he went behind the house to the privy and they then settled with his wife and Ikey.

We didn't speak all the way back home, where my mother was up and about, feeding the baby. Pa gave her a brief outline of what had occurred, leaving out the gorier details. Even so, it was the hell of a shock for her. She sat down suddenly, as though her knees had given way and she had been struck all of a heap.

'Where will this matter end now, Ebenezer?' she enquired listlessly. 'I knew that there would be more killing. Do you then propose to set here and wait until your own family have fallen prey to these bloodthirsty assassins?'

'I shall go into the town after we hold Al's funeral, Martha. My purpose will be to rouse the folk living there to a sense of their own danger and culpability if they remain silent in the face of such goings on. Their interests are lined up with ours; Anderson and his men will not bring prosperity to Zion, but will bring about its destruction. This sort of thing has a habit of spreading, and before you know it men in town will be shot for some trifling cause. I shall explain this to them.'

Nothing Ma and I could say would dissuade my father from what even at that age, I could see was a rash enterprise. He was determined that as soon as Al and his

family were buried he would try to win over the town of
Zion to his own point of view. In the meantime, he purposed to ride around and inform our neighbours of
these latest developments. 'And I should not wonder,' he
said soberly, 'If one or two men hereabouts now think
that it is time for them to dig up and leave. Anderson has
saved hisself the trouble and expense of paying their
passage home. Killing Al and his family was a right smart
move, you see. So far, this has not cost him one cent in
cash money.'

I seldom heard my father speak in such a bitter way.
Ma went over and put her arm round his shoulders.
'Don't take on so, Ebenezer. I should not like this business to make you in anyways embittered.' They stood for
a moment together like that, and for a brief moment I
could see them not as my ma and pa, but as they must
once have been; two young lovers who were tender and
close. This cast them in a new and strange light to me. I
did not like to think of them so and thrust the thought
from me as though there were something smutty and
unclean about it. This was a shame, because I never again
saw them look so close and loving. I should have
savoured that moment for all it was worth.

Later that day my father rode into Zion and
acquainted the minister at the church with what had
taken place. He desired him to notify the authorities in
the nearest big town of the affair, which the minister
promised to do. You must know that there was no telegraph office in Zion, and only an irregular and erratic
postal service. There was little point in sending messages
seeking the aid of a marshal. By the time the message was

received and a man dispatched, matters would probably have resolved themselves one way or another already.

It was fixed that my father would bury Al and Ikey and his mother on the second day following their deaths. He went over to their place and tidied things up a bit, prepared the bodies for burial and engaged a couple of the neighbours to help him dig the grave. It seemed easier to dig one big hole, rather than three little ones. That may sound a mite disrespectful, but all these men had farms to tend and were also riding patrol after dark. It was just easier to dig the one hole, that was all.

Now it is a strange thing, but I cannot for the very life of me recall the name of Ikey's mother. This is a terrible thing, really, because I am surely the only body alive now on the face of God's earth who remembers that woman or who even met her. And now I can't even recollect her name! This has, I think, less to do with my advancing age and is more because I always thought of her as either Ikey's ma or Al's wife. What a sad epitaph is that, for a woman to be remembered only as somebody's wife or mother!

At Al's funeral there was no longer any nonsense about men not carrying firearms. After the unfortunate goings on at Tom Dillon's graveside nobody felt inclined to take any chances and all the men had pistols strapped to their belts, a couple had also brought rifles and shotguns, which they kept close at hand. There was a definite feeling that we were under siege. My father once again read the burial service for the dead and then closed the Bible and set it to one side. He cleared his throat and spoke.

' "Vengeance is mine, saith the Lord, I will repay." By which I take it that the Good Book does not want us to seek revenge for any wrongs which we might have received. I tell you folks here gathered that Al was the staunchest friend a man could have and that in the short time I knew him, he came to the aid of me and mine on more than one occasion.' Pa looked over at me when he said this. 'Nevertheless, I shall not seek to avenge myself upon the cowards who carried out this bloodthirsty attack. I shall instead go into town two days from now and acquaint as many there as possible with what has taken place. I owe this, anyway, to Al. You are all knowing that after Tom Dillon was killed, a rumour was set round Zion that it was as a consequence of some trouble with another man's wife. I will not have those sorts of lies spoken uncontested about the man we have just buried. If I have to stand on the street corners of the town and declaim on this matter, I shall do so. I will seek to bring those responsible to justice.'

Even these many years later, the events that I am now about to relate still have a raw and painful feeling to them. Still and all, having begun, I shall finish.

My father had announced his intention of going to Zion and telling all the townsfolk what a murdering scoundrel was this man Anderson, who portrayed himself there in the light of a leading citizen. Nothing that my mother or I could say would move him and he rode around the neighbouring farms and declared his purpose again, as he had at the funeral, inviting others to join with him in this enterprise. There was, as far as I gathered from what he said, no appetite for the idea.

Having seen two homesteaders murdered in cold blood, to say nothing of Al's wife and stepson, the general view was that Anderson would stop at nothing until he had driven us all from the area. You may believe it or not, but some were blaming my father for the deaths, saying that they might have reached an accommodation with Anderson, were it not for my father's stiff-necked and proud ways. In the end, not one man offered to ride into town with Pa and so, two days after Al's funeral, he rode alone towards Zion.

I was not witness to what I am about to describe, but heard later from those who had seen it. I must, before telling what befell, say a few words about the Mayes brothers, one of whom was Georgia Jack. They were both half-Cherokee Indian and very practised in the Indian arts of concealment and ambush. It was Joel Mayes, you will recall, who taught these things to Quantrill, the bandit leader. One trick that Quantrill and his men got up to was dressing as Union troops and in this way being able to get right up close to Union soldiers before, unexpectedly and without warning, opening fire upon them. Such conduct put them on the level of cowardly assassins rather than true soldiers. I have explained somewhat of the Mayes brothers' mode of action, because it has bearing upon what happened later.

We know what fate struck my Pa because the owner of the general store was on his roof that morning, fixing a leak. I have told you that the land in that part of Nebraska is very flat, which means that you can see clear to the horizon. This is what the man on the roof saw.

A man on horseback was approaching the outskirts of

Zion at a walk. He was perhaps a mile outside the town. Coming along behind him were two other men, also on horseback. They were moving a little faster, probably at a smart trot. The scene looked peaceable and the man in front did not stop or seem to take any action as the other two riders came up behind him. He was clearly not alarmed, which suggests that they smiled or otherwise signalled that their intentions were peaceful. As the two men looked to be about to overtake the man, the sound of shooting erupted. The lone rider fell from his horse, which then bolted. Then the two riders, who had been coming from behind, wheeled round and made off back the way they had come at a gallop.

When the shots rang out people walking in the streets of Zion stopped and looked round uneasily. They sensed that some new devilment was afoot. Looking towards where the shooting seemed to have come from, a rider-less horse could be seen standing by itself and doing nothing much. Once it looked as though the shooting had stopped, a couple of fellows went to see what was what and to fetch the horse into town. As they approached it, one of them recognized it as the palomino bought by my father. The men found not only the horse, grazing quietly, but a dead man, shot in the back several times. It was my father.

Me and my mother were sitting outside the house after Pa had ridden into town, wondering what the outcome would be. I think that we were both expecting him to come back a little low and discouraged because nobody in the town would take his warnings seriously. For my part, I was getting ready to sympathize with and encourage him. I was also feeling guilty about what a trial I had lately been to him and resolving privately that I would change my ways and make him proud of me.

A rider appeared over the ridge behind the house and for a moment I thought it was Pa returning. The rider came on, the horse walking at a slow pace, as though the rider were not over-anxious to reach his destination. Leastways, he was not urging the beast on or nothing. As he came nigh to us, I saw that it was the man who owned the livery stable. A sudden terror took ahold of me and I jumped up and ran to meet him.

As soon as I looked into his face close up, I knew at once that my father was dead. This jovial and often inebriate man looked haggard, as though he hardly knew what he was to say to us. Ma was watching; she did not appear to have caught on as quickly as I had myself to the new situation in which we found ourselves. I went right up close to Mr Carter and said in a low voice, 'Tell me quickly, is he dead?' He just nodded his head sadly. I said, 'Was he murdered?' and Mr Carter nodded once more. 'Leave us be then. I will tell my mother.' He said nothing, but just turned his horse round and began plodding off back the way he had come.

You are at this point very likely thinking: *Well, how could the child be so self-possessed at such news? Surely she must have a heart of stone?* Nothing of the sort, is my reply to that. I was almost borne down with grief at hearing this, but knew that no purpose would be served by wailing and weeping. I went back to my mother, who was looking at me with fear in her eyes. I sat down, put my arm round her and told her what had happened.

The two of us sat there crying and clinging on to each other like shipwrecked mariners for a time, until Davy woke up and began to howl. I tended to him while my mother just stared blankly at the river, as though she just had no idea what to do next. As for me, I was already making some plans in my head. I was saving my grief for a more convenient season, seeing that we would not be able to stay here for very long without my father to protect us. I had no illusions at all as to the likely sequence of events if we did not leave pretty sharpish. It would entail a midnight visit from a bunch of ruffians, with the possibility of rape and murder being involved.

The first thing I purposed to do was to act as though I were the man of the house now and to help my mother in her sorrow. That might sound a strange thing to say, but I suppose that my father treating me as he had done had given me an odd idea as to my place in the scheme of things. I did not act like many a young girl would under such circumstances. The first step was to get my father's things from town and to make some arrangements with a view to leaving the district, before we fell prey to the kind of troubles which I talk of above.

I did not like to leave my mother alone, but explained to her that I must go and fetch Pa's horse and see about other things. I was also wondering what on earth we would be doing about a funeral. Presumably, I would have to organize that as well.

I walked to Zion alone. I considered taking the shotgun with me, but for several reasons decided against this course of action. Chief of these reasons was that I had a plan at the back of my mind and wished for everybody to see me now in the light of a heartbroken and helpless young girl. I did not think that this impression was likely to be strengthened if I turned up in town with a twelve-gauge tucked under my arm!

At the livery stable I found the owner, still shaken by this sudden death. I said to him, 'I am sorry to be a nuisance, but I will need to make some arrangements with regard to burying my father and suchlike. Also where my mother and me will have to leave the area now.'

Mr Carter nodded sympathetically. 'Yes, yes, I see that. I shall help as I am able. What is it that you wish?'

'I must first see about burying my father. Before that though, I must have his horse, pistol and any other effects. What am I to do?'

The man stared at me as though he could hardly believe that he was hearing such a young girl being so businesslike about a great personal tragedy of this nature. Bearing in mind that it was not much above two hours since I had first received news of the death, I suppose he thought that I would have been prostrate with grief and unable to function in any respect. This was not however my way, even as a child.

I will not weary readers with every detail of what I said and did while I was in town. It is enough that I arranged for the burial to take place at the church in two days and that I let it be widely known that we were going to cut and run, returning East as soon as my father was in the ground. If you are wondering why I agreed to my father being buried in the local churchyard, it is because he himself was not sentimental about dead bodies. As far as I could gauge, he had been promoted to glory and the empty husk that remained had no part of his new existence. On a practical level, there was no percentage in paying to have the body carted out to our land, since we would anyway be leaving, just as soon as I had tended to what remained to be done.

When I got back to our house, my mother had been busying herself with domestic matters to take her mind off the grief. I offered her the idea that we should now consider taking any offer of help which her parents were minded to make to us. The problem was contacting them, there not being much of a mail service between Zion and anywhere else much. I elicited from her the information that her father's business had a telegraphic address and made plans to pay somebody to travel to the nearest office and send a message, preparing my grandparents for our arrival.

'What will become of us, Maybelle, without your father to care for us?' said Ma. I had no real answer to this question, but responded with a variety of meaningless platitudes. I was, I suppose, in a better frame of mind than my mother in some ways, because I at least had an aim, something which I intended to undertake relating to my father's murder. This gave me a strength and purpose which allowed me to defer my grief until it would not interfere with what I planned.

'Hey Ma,' I said, 'you know he is walking the streets of glory this very minute and perhaps looking down on us. We must not grudge him the joy of being with his Lord.' Ma nodded her head and looked a fraction cheered by this. Like I say, meaningless platitudes, although such things have their uses, I guess, at such times.

'You just set there, Ma,' said I, 'and I will undertake all that is needful. We must remember Davy and not surrender ourselves to grief for his sake. He needs us now.'

'Maybelle, it is times like this that I see you are become a young woman and are no longer a child. It sorrows me that we have not always been on such terms.'

I did not know what to say to this, except to rest my hand on her shoulder and then embrace her. I would think on my relationship with her as well at a later date. Really, all that I wished then in my secret heart was to get her and little Davy out of the way, so that I could be avenged upon the cowardly men who had organized my father's murder.

CHAPTER 13

It says in the Bible, *Morning brings counsel*, which is to say that after sleeping you sometimes have a clearer view of problems and how they are to be remedied. This was certainly the case on this occasion, because the second I woke up, my whole plan was clear in my mind. Davy woke and I gave him somewhat to eat and drink, letting my mother continue to slumber. When she woke I made breakfast for her as well and then told her, 'Ma, I'm going into town again. Write down all the details about your folks in Boston and I will engage to send word to them. They must know of our misfortunes and perhaps will send us money or tickets for the railroad. Otherwise, it is not plain to me how we shall reach Boston from here.'

'My father is not a poor man,' said Ma. 'He will provide for us when once he knows what has befallen us.'

Every so often I would suddenly think about my father and the pain would be like an animal clawing against my belly. I would have to clench my muscles and set my face hard, just in order not to start sobbing and giving myself

146

up to sorrow. This I could not yet do, at least until I had settled the matter that was in my mind. It was nursing that plan that protected me from the worst of the grief. It gave me an aim and I held the idea in my heart as a comfort.

In town I wandered around in a distracted fashion, causing people to remark in hushed coices, 'Poor child, she is broken down by this tragedy,' and similar sympathetic things. The man in the general store put me in contact with somebody who was travelling to a way station on the railroad and undertook to send a telegraph message for me. I saw one or two of Anderson's cowboys who marked me narrowly, obviously under the impression that soon Ebenezer Cade and his family would all be out of the cart and they could get on with terrorizing the remaining homesteaders without a strong and principled man to stand up on their behalf. I went over to them, looking as defeated and wore out as I could, which did not require a great deal of acting, and handed them a letter I had written, desiring them to pass it unopened to their boss. I emphasized that it was a matter of business and that they would be in trouble with Anderson if they interfered in any wise with it. The man whom I gave it to said nothing, but looked at me as though he could not work out the play. Then he nodded, tucked it into his shirt and intimated to me that he would be sure to pass it on. I did not wish either the homesteaders or anybody else well at that time, remembering that they had not appreciated all that my father was attempting to do for them.

I made sure that I was observed throughout the town

in my chosen role of helpless girl. Some little while after the events which I am relating, I found myself placed in a Catholic school and I heard that the motto of the Jesuits, a bunch of monks, is to this effect: *When the end is lawful, the means are likewise lawful.* Which is pretty much to say that if you feel that undertaking an enterprise is the right thing to do, then any actions you are obliged to take are justified by that end. This is a roundabout way of saying that although I was in reality almost struck down in a heap by grief for my pa, I did not scruple to 'lay it on thick' and act up that part. I had my reasons, as you will shortly see.

Having made all necessary arrangements, I trudged back to our house. I told Ma, 'We have just over twenty dollars in cash money. This should be enough to get us to a town with a bank. If your folks in Boston can tele-graph to the town, we can collect money in this wise from a bank and make our way onwards.'

'I am sure that this will work,' said my mother. 'You are a tower of strength to me in this time, Maybelle, and even though your own heart must be breaking, you are bearing up and helping me. It will not be forgotten.'

I felt a bit uncomfortable like, being spoken to so. I was, after all, deceiving my mother to some extent and not quite being the obedient daughter she was now viewing me as. I changed the subject. 'Do you think we can pack everything away today? We will not have further need of a wagon and oxen. I have told a man in Zion that we will sell them there. This should bring us some more money to tide us by.'

'Is there anything that you have not thought on,

Maybelle? You are a regular marvel.'

'The burying will take place tomorrow morning. That preacher has said that he will not charge us for this. He will say some few words and when that is complete, we can leave town. I think that somebody will take us to where we can get the train.'

'I have had some rough things to say to you in recent weeks. I will say now that I was wrong. You are all that your pa thought you were and more.'

'How would it be if we were to take all the belongings we will be heading East with and leave others things here? I do not look for us to be needing a shotgun if we are going to live in a big city. Perhaps we could get you and Davy settled in town and then I can come back here and give out those things which we will not be wanting, to the neighbouring farms? I am sure that Pa would have wanted things to be so.'

I felt guilty invoking my dead father's name in this way, not to mention where the entire things sounded awful thin to me even as I said it. Ma though, did not notice anything amiss and took it to be but one more instance of my new and responsible character.

I packed some of our stuff together and placed it in the wagon. The funeral was due to take place the next day and I had to prepare everything just in the right way beforehand.

Here is what I had not told my mother. We were due to leave town as soon as my father was interred. The timing was important and I was hoping that it would all work according to my plan. The train could be signalled to stop at a little way-halt some few miles south of Zion.

It should reach there around 5 p.m. The funeral was due for eleven o'clock and we would need to be out of town to be sure of catching the train eastward, no later than three o'clock. In my letter to Anderson I had engaged to meet him at our property promptly at two o'clock. I had assured him that we were leaving and offered to sign over to him our claim to the land for $500. This sounded even to my young ears, a pretty feeble and ridiculous notion, but I was counting on his not wanting to leave any loose ends and turning up, if for no other reason, out of pure curiosity. The timing was cut damn fine, but I thought that if I did not waste any time I would be able to achieve my purpose in the given time.

The day dawned bright and we were all up and ready at dawn. I hitched up the oxen to the wagon, left one or two things in the soddy, and we headed into town. I knew that it would probably take longer than I had planned for, which is why I wanted to leave early. I believe that I have already mentioned that oxen are among the slowest creatures on God's earth and it would have been quicker to crawl into Zion on our hands and knees than travel like this. Still and all, I had sold the wagon and beasts and we would need the money to tide us over until we made contact with my mother's folks in Boston. I had already sold Dollar back to Mr Carter of the livery stable. I was hoping that my grandparents were as well off as Ma claimed, because otherwise I could not foresee what would become of our family.

The funeral took but twenty minutes. I suppose that, because the minister was giving his services for free, he aimed to keep it to a minimum. Three people from the town attended, as did one or two others. Ma and I did not have much to say afterwards. I had spoken to Mr Carter at the livery stable and he said that my mother could sit with his wife until it was time for us to go to the railroad. The man buying the wagon and oxen met me at the stable and paid for them, which was a great relief to me.

At around 12.30, I said to Ma, 'I have to go back out to the house now, like I told you. The man giving us a ride in his buggy will be here at three o'clock or there-abouts. Be sure that you are ready to leave because we are cutting the time fine.'

'Would it not be better to leave earlier, then?' enquired my mother anxiously.

'No, it will be fine,' I assured her. 'Just be ready to leave at three o'clock.'

I then set off at a fair pace towards our soddy. I was lucky, because nobody from the town seemed to mark me and I was able to slip away more or less unnoticed. I did not think that Anderson would want to be hanging round waiting for me and so I was tolerably sure he would not get there much before two o'clock. I still wanted to have time in hand before he arrived, to prepare. I walked for twenty yards and then ran the next twenty and so reached our soddy by what I calculated was perhaps 1.15.

I had never had the intention of giving out any of our belongings to any of the other homesteaders; this had just been a ruse to explain my absence for an hour or two to my mother. Once I reached the house I took down the shotgun, which was still hanging on the wall. I had the flask of powder with me and also the little tin box of percussion caps. The piece was still loaded, but at some point my father must have removed the caps for safety. I put new ones over the nipples and then went outside. I scooped up a handful of soil and grit from Ma's little patch where she had begun a vegetable garden and added this to the charge of buckshot that I knew was already in there. I tore a couple of fragments off my petticoat to provide wadding and rammed the whole home carefully. I minded what my father had told me about such material making any wound a deadly one. I did not want to make any error with what I was about.

I guessed that Anderson would be coming up the valley, riding towards the side of our house, so I went round the other side, sat down and waited out of sight. I was thinking that, at a guess, Anderson would turn up with only one other man. How dangerous could a girl my age be to him, would be his thinking. His plan would be to fob me off with fifty dollars or so and try to get my signature on some document or other. He would then be after pulling down this house that we'd built and returning the area to prairie.

I had been sitting there for half an hour or so when I heard the sound of hoofs, as what sounded like two or three horses came heading towards the house. I stood up carefully, making sure that nobody would be able to see me, and waited. As the riders came closer I edged round the corner of the house so that I was at the back of it. Now the riders were right at the front of our soddy and I was standing at the back.

There was a jingling of spurs as men dismounted. One

called out,

'Hallo in there!' There was a pause during which he had evidently gone inside and had a look. Then he said, 'Ain't nobody here and they stuff's mostly gone. Looks like they lit out. No sign of that girl though.'

I recognized Anderson's voice as he replied,

'What did you expect?'

'What she playing at, writing to you in that way? You think she coming?'

I recognized Jack Mayes's voice. It struck me that matters could hardly have turned out better and that only those two men had come. I cocked both hammers of the shotgun and raised it to my shoulder, ready to fire.

Mayes said, 'You wanna pull this pile of shit down now?'

'Hell, no. I'll get a few of the boys to ride over later.'

I walked slowly round the side of the house. Anderson and Mayes were both standing there, maybe six feet away. Anderson had his back to me, but Jack Mayes, he saw me at once. I was glad, I wanted them to see me first.

'Hidy!' I said.

'Ah, shit!' he exclaimed when he found himself looking down the muzzle of my gun. Anderson turned round in surprise and Mayes told him in a low, urgent voice, like *he* was the boss suddenly, 'Just don't move, you hear me? She's got us covered good.'

Anderson looked at me and I could tell that it affronted his pride to have his foreman speak so to him in front of me. Nor did he take overmuch to me pointing a gun at him. He stared at me contemptuously, saying, 'Hell, she's only a kid.' Then he reached unhurriedly for the revolver hanging at his waist. When Jack Mayes saw this he moaned,

'Oh, Christ, no, no. . . .'

His words were cut off abruptly when I fired one barrel straight into Anderson's belly, aiming low to compensate for the recoil, just as Pa had told me to. We were that close that the blast knocked him flying, to say nothing of blowing a large hole in his stomach. The boom of the shotgun echoed back and forth across the valley like rolling thunder, and before it had died down I turned to Mayes and let him have the other barrel. I fired at once, without bothering to lower my aim and the result was that the shot caught him much higher than the one that hit Anderson. He took the full force of it in his face and throat, dropping dead at my feet. Anderson was lying there with various parts of his intestines exposed and steaming gently. He wasn't quite dead, but it surely would not be long. His eyes was open and he were looking towards me. I went up close, leaned over and said, 'That was for my pa.' Then I spat on him.

I rushed down to the river and threw the shotgun into the water. Then I set off for town, doing that same walking and then running pace. I didn't expect anybody to be that keen on rushing to investigate gunfire after all that had been going on. With luck, I would not encounter anybody at all on the way back to Zion, and so it proved.

The church clock told me that it lacked twenty minutes to three o'clock and so my timing had been pretty well perfect. I skipped along to the home of the livery stable owner and knocked on the door. Ma was ready and waiting and just then the buggy drew up and we loaded our bags on the back. Then, after hugs and kisses from Mrs Carter, we shook the dust of that place from our feet and were soon speeding along the dirt track leading to the railroad line.

CHAPTER 14

Now I suppose that you will want to know a bit about what happened after all these dramatic incidents. Well, the first thing I can tell you is that after shooting Anderson and Mayes and getting clear of the area and on the train with my mother and baby brother, I broke down in tears like any normal girl of that age and was nigh on inconsolable for the loss of my beloved father. The planning of my vengeance had enabled me to arrange getting us out of that place without falling apart entirely, but once I had accomplished it, I was relieved of the need to be so strong and could seek comfort in my mother's arms. I don't believe killing those two scoundrels caused me any lasting harm of a psychological nature.

My grandparents turned out to be as wealthy as Ma had represented them to be and they lived in a big house with servants, running water and every sort of convenience one could hope for. They were rejoiced to see their daughter again and even seemed pleased to see me initially. However, it did not take long for them to discover that I was next door to being a perfect heathen, with manners and behaviour that might answer on the trail but was not what they wanted to see on the streets of Boston. The consequence was that I was packed off to a most exclusive Catholic boarding school, where the nuns endeavoured to make a good Christian woman of me. The less said about that episode of my life, the better!

What came of my murders, you are most likely wondering? Well I will tell you that I never breathed a word about that matter from that day to this. I did not tell my mother, nor my husband, when once I had managed to catch one. Nor either did I tell my children of it. For ninety years, I have kept my own counsel on the matter. I have of late felt that I should at least set out some record of the business, even if I do not directly tell any living soul of it. I have found myself thinking over the events of that far off time and wondering if I behaved as I should have done. Not that I have any bad conscience about shooting down those two men I killed. I would cheerfully do the same again tomorrow. I wonder more about whether I was inadvertently the cause of Al's and his family's deaths, to say nothing of my own father. There is not much I could do anyway about it at this late stage and I guess that a child of that age was bound to make some mischief in those circumstances.

I heard later some scraps of information about what happened out in Nebraska after we left. The death of Anderson and Mayes was what you might describe as the final act in the tragedy. Zion had about had enough of shooting and bloodshed, as had everybody else. Nobody asked particularly who had killed him and his foreman. I guess the homesteaders could have made a shrewd guess, but they weren't about to talk of the matter.

Anderson had some relatives come from somewhere to rake over his property: his concerns got split up and an accommodation was reached with various of the small farmers. These relatives did not wish to continue any sort of vendetta and blood feud, being content with taking a share of the dead man's estate, which was considerable. I have never seen any mention of this little affair in any books about that time. When all's said and done, it involved only half a dozen deaths, which was not a considerable number. Of course any death is a tragedy, but with the thousands and thousands who died in the war, just a few years before that, six or seven deaths were nothing to think too much of.

My grandparents were, as I have intimated, scandalized at my general ignorance and wild ways. The school did not succeed overmuch in taming me. I had best not relate all the steps in my fall from grace, which ultimately resulted in the reverend mother sending a despairing telegram to my grandfather, desiring him to make urgent arrangements to remove me from the school at once.

We have almost reached the conclusion of my tale. You will by now, if you have been paying heed to what I have been saying that is, realize why the yellow ribbon that my father bought me that day in 1875 is so precious to me even now. It is because this was the last thing he ever did buy me and that a brief time before his death. I have kept it safe and treasured it for almost a century now.

What then of my own present life? Well, I have to tell you that my impression is that it is fast drawing to a close.

I suppose you will be saying to yourselves, *Hell's afire, the crazy old woman is one hundred and five years old and realizes that her life is almost over? That ain't exactly needing any sort of ability to foretell the future!* It is more than that, though. I did not imbibe much in the way of book-learning from the nuns at the school which my grandparents sent me. That is, as one might aptly say, understating the case to a considerable extent! One thing I do recollect though and that was being made to read a poem called *The Ancient Mariner*. In it was an old and half-crazy man who was under a curse to grab hold of strangers and tell them his life's history. He would accost some hapless bystander and insist that he set still while the old sailor related to him the story of his adventures at sea. For some reason, this long poem took my fancy and I read it over and again.

As you all might have guessed, I am currently resident in what is termed a retirement home. There being little enough in the way of entertainment here, I have taken to reading a lot lately. I got one of the staff to hunt down a copy of that *Ancient Mariner* poem for me, which I have not read for years, and it affected me even more deeply than it did when I was a girl. The old man, he could have no peace until he had told his tale and that is the restlessness that has been upon me too, lately. I did not want to tell this story to a real live person and so writing it down in this way has been the next best thing. Setting all of that event down like this on paper has done me a power of good, almost like confessing to a priest or some such. At any rate, I feel a burden has been lifted from me. I have a feeling that I shall rest easier in my bed tonight for doing so.

This then is the true and full account of how I was on the trail in that far off year of 1875 and how it ended in my committing murder not once but twice.

29 July 1965